REKI KAWAHARA   ABEC   BEE-PEE

SWORD ART ONLINE 25
unital ring IV

SAO
SWORD ART ONLINE

"*Shagyuoooooo!!*"

§ The Life Harvester

A freakish monster that lives up to its name. Its mammoth form is reminiscent of the Skullreaper, a boss that devastated the frontline players on the seventy-fifth floor of Aincrad.

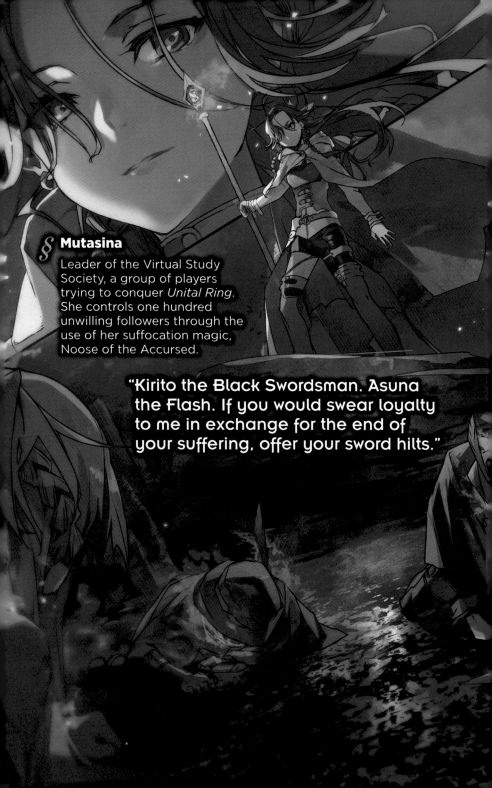

§ Mutasina

Leader of the Virtual Study Society, a group of players trying to conquer *Unital Ring*. She controls one hundred unwilling followers through the use of her suffocation magic, Noose of the Accursed.

"Kirito the Black Swordsman. Asuna the Flash. If you would swear loyalty to me in exchange for the end of your suffering, offer your sword hilts."

So this is as far as we get.

§ **Kirito**

The boy who beat *SAO* and brought peace to the Underworld. He and his friends built the town of Ruis na Ríg on their quest to conquer *Unital Ring*.

"I'm so happy we got the chance to meet again!"

§ Stica

The descendant of Tiese Schtrinen, who served as Eugeo's page two centuries ago. Like Laurannei, she is a member of the Integrity Pilots, who protect the safety of the Underworld.

§ Alice

An Integrity Knight from the Underworld—and the world's first true bottom-up artificial intelligence. Even two centuries later, she is still known as the Osmanthus Knight in the Underworld.

"Lady Alice, Lady Asuna, Sir Kirito, it's so good to see you!"

§ **Laurannei**

The descendant of Ronie Arabel, who served as Kirito's page two centuries ago. A member of the Integrity Pilots, serving under Commander Eolyne Herlentz.

§ **Asuna**

Kirito's girlfriend. She once fought in the Underworld's great war as Stacia, Goddess of Creation, and is now referred to by the title of Star Queen.

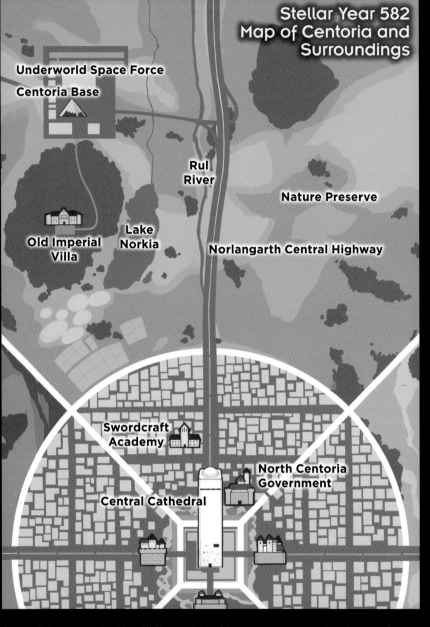

**Stellar Year 582
Map of Centoria and
Surroundings**

Underworld Space Force

Centoria Base

Rul
River

Nature Preserve

Old Imperial
Villa

Lake
Norkia

Norlangarth Central Highway

Swordcraft
Academy

North Centoria
Government

Central Cathedral

A small town created by Kirito and his friends to serve as the base of their adventures in the world of *Unital Ring*. Known by the nickname Kirito Town. Kirito and Asuna's log cabin is at the center, enclosed by a circular wall that is about sixty yards in diameter, with four quadrants surrounding the cabin to the north, south, east, and west.

Illustration: Reki Kawahara

SWORD ART ONLINE unital ring IV

VOLUME 25

Reki Kawahara

abec

bee-pee

YEN ON

NEW YORK

SWORD ART ONLINE, Volume 25: UNITAL RING IV
REKI KAWAHARA

Translation by Stephen Paul
Cover art by abec

SWORD ART ONLINE Vol.25
©Reki Kawahara 2020
Edited by Dengeki Bunko
First published in Japan in 2020 by KADOKAWA CORPORATION, Tokyo.
English translation rights arranged with KADOKAWA CORPORATION, Tokyo, through Tuttle-Mori Agency, Inc., Tokyo.

English translation © 2022 by Yen Press, LLC

Yen On
150 West 30th Street, 19th Floor
New York, NY 10001

Visit us at yenpress.com
facebook.com/yenpress
twitter.com/yenpress
yenpress.tumblr.com
instagram.com/yenpress

First Yen On Edition: August 2022
Edited by Thalia Sutton & Yen On Editorial: Payton Campbell
Designed by Yen Press Design: Andy Swist

Yen On is an imprint of Yen Press, LLC.
The Yen On name and logo are trademarks of Yen Press, LLC.

Library of Congress Cataloging-in-Publication Data
Names: Kawahara, Reki, author. | Abec, 1985– illustrator. | Paul, Stephen, translator.
Title: Sword art online / Reki Kawahara, abec ; translation, Stephen Paul.
Description: First Yen On edition. | New York, NY : Yen On, 2014–
Identifiers: LCCN 2014001175 | ISBN 9780316371247 (v. 1 : pbk.) |
    ISBN 9780316376815 (v. 2 : pbk.) | ISBN 9780316296427 (v. 3 : pbk.) |
    ISBN 9780316296434 (v. 4 : pbk.) | ISBN 9780316296441 (v. 5 : pbk.) |
    ISBN 9780316296458 (v. 6 : pbk.) | ISBN 9780316390408 (v. 7 : pbk.) |
    ISBN 9780316390415 (v. 8 : pbk.) | ISBN 9780316390422 (v. 9 : pbk.) |
    ISBN 9780316390439 (v. 10 : pbk.) | ISBN 9780316390446 (v. 11 : pbk.) |
    ISBN 9780316390453 (v. 12 : pbk.) | ISBN 9780316390460 (v. 13 : pbk.) |
    ISBN 9780316390484 (v. 14 : pbk.) | ISBN 9780316390491 (v. 15 : pbk.) |
    ISBN 9781975304188 (v. 16 : pbk.) | ISBN 9781975356972 (v. 17 : pbk.) |
    ISBN 9781975356996 (v. 18 : pbk.) | ISBN 9781975357016 (v. 19 : pbk.) |
    ISBN 9781975357030 (v. 20 : pbk.) | ISBN 9781975315955 (v. 21 : pbk.) |
    ISBN 9781975321741 (v. 22 : pbk.) | ISBN 9781975321765 (v. 23 : pbk.) |
    ISBN 9781975321789 (v. 24 : pbk.) | ISBN 9781975343408 (v. 25 : pbk.)
Subjects: CYAC: Science fiction. | BISAC: FICTION / Science Fiction / Adventure.
Classification: pz7.K1755Ain 2014 | DDC [Fic]—dc23
LC record available at https://lccn.loc.gov/2014001175

ISBNs: 978-1-9753-4340-8 (paperback)
      978-1-9753-4341-5 (ebook)

10 9 8 7 6 5 4 3 2 1

LSC-C

Printed in the United States of America

"THIS MIGHT BE A GAME, BUT IT'S NOT SOMETHING YOU PLAY."

—Akihiko Kayaba, *Sword Art Online* programmer

SWORD ART ONLINE unital ring IV

Reki Kawahara

abec

bee-pee

1

There were many boss monsters lurking in the floating castle of Aincrad, the setting of the VRMMORPG *Sword Art Online*.

They could be broadly split into two groups: field bosses, who guarded certain choke points in the wilderness of each floor, and floor bosses, who waited on the top floor of the labyrinth tower that led to each consecutive floor. The particularly dangerous bosses were given unique enemy names, which used *the* in the title. Therefore, despite the potential confusion, players ended up calling them The Bosses.

Fewer players knew, however, that there was an even higher rank to be found among those unique bosses.

There was, for example, the field boss of the fifty-fifth floor, X'rphan the White Wyrm, that knocked Lisbeth and me down a deep pit. The floor boss of the seventy-fourth floor that I fought with Asuna and Klein, however, was the Gleameyes. The former had a proper name before its epithet, but the latter was just a composite descriptive name. So all The Bosses could be divided into those with proper names and without.

You would assume that the ones with proper names would be the more powerful of the two, but in fact, it was the reverse. This was because the bosses without proper names were actually so feared, the story went, that their proper names were never spoken—and lost to time.

As a matter of fact, nearly all the boss monsters that made me think "I might die right now" were in that category. That included the blue-eyed demon, the Gleameyes; the Fatal Scythe, underground on the first floor; and the floor boss that laid waste to the best players in the game on the seventy-fifth floor.

That boss's name: the Skullreaper.

The title of that dreaded foe came to mind now, still wreathed in the fear and sweat of the past. "Asuna…," I murmured, "does it look like what I think it does…?"

Still on the ground, she whispered back, "Yes…It's not a skeleton, and it's about twice as big…But that's the boss of the seventy-fifth floor…"

If we both had the same reaction, then it couldn't be a mere coincidence.

The monstrous beast staring down at us from across the stormy night plain was a modified version of the Skullreaper.

It was a sixty-foot-long centipede with the face of a man. From the body, sheathed in gleaming black carapace and rippling muscle, sprang countless legs. The tail was as sharp as a spear, and the two front legs were huge, curved scythes. Its elongated head featured four shining red eyes and a gaping mouth that opened in all four directions.

The spindle-shaped cursor hanging over the man-faced centipede featured three HP bars with a name written in English: *the Life Harvester*. If you tore off the shell and muscle from this creature, it would indeed look exactly like the Skullreaper—although as Asuna said, the size was very different.

"Is this supposed to mean it fell out of the seventy-fifth floor when Aincrad crashed to earth…?" I gaped.

Asuna shook her head. "Remember? Argo said that thing was chasing her for at least fifteen miles. That's way too far, and it also doesn't explain why that one has flesh and armor."

"Yeah…I guess that's true," I replied. "Plus, all the floor bosses in New Aincrad have been altered from their *SAO* forms."

As I spoke, there came a hideous, screeching roar, like boulders grinding against one another.

"Jyashuaaaa!"

As though drawn by the Life Harvester's call, purple lightning darted across the black sky, revealing the monster with scythes raised. A deep, cracking rumble arrived moments later. The rain had stopped falling at some point, but the lightning wasn't finished, it seemed.

"Kirito, what should we do?!" shouted Alice, who had fallen back a short distance away. Our other companions—Lisbeth, Leafa, Silica, Sinon, Argo, Yui, Klein, Agil, his wife, Hyme, the nineteen other *Insectsite* players with her, Misha the thornspike cave bear, and Kuro the lapispine dark panther—were all waiting for my decision.

Fight or flight?

It didn't seem like a foe that could be beaten, to be honest. Alongside me, Alice, Lisbeth, and the rhinoceros and stag beetles from *Insectsite* had all guarded against the Life Harvester's right scythe swing, and all five of us were easily smashed off our feet. My iron breastplate and left gauntlet were brutally cracked, and I had lost nearly 60 percent of my hit points. The others were similarly damaged.

The scythe swing did not have any shining light effects—it was an ordinary attack. Five of us were unable to block a mere basic attack, which suggested that there was a massive statistical abyss between us, one that player skill could not make up. If we challenged it again and again and perfectly learned its patterns, we might be able to beat it—but that was not how *Unital Ring* worked. If we died even once, we would be forever banished from this world.

We ought to flee. Assuming that was even possible.

But even that would be difficult. If it was true that Argo had been running for nearly twenty miles, the Life Harvester was gifted with an almost impossibly stubborn pursuit algorithm for a video game monster. There would only be two ways to throw off a monster like this: flee to a location it couldn't reach or foist it off on another player.

To do the former, we'd need to get on top of a sheer cliff or head into a cave, or perhaps a system-protected town, but we were surrounded by forest and plains for miles, plus Kirito Town—Ruis na Ríg, I had to remind myself—was a town we'd built ourselves, meaning there were no system barriers to keep the monsters out. We couldn't choose the latter option because there was no one else around, not that I would want to make such a choice in the first place.

The Life Harvester lowered its scythes and began to move this way, its many legs rhythmically undulating. There was no time to mull it over. If I didn't choose between fight or flight now, we'd all be wiped out.

The mental mention of the word *wiped* sent a horrid chill through me. It felt as though the insides of my avatar had turned to ice.

If only I knew the monster's attack patterns. If only.

This voiceless cry raced through my mind, flashing into white sparks that burst like fireworks.

Wait a minute. Should I know them already? If the Life Harvester was just the Skullreaper with flesh and armor on top, then Asuna and I had fought it once before. It was nearly two years ago, but tangible memories of battling on the brink of death did not fade quickly.

"Asuna!" I shouted, grabbing her fragile shoulder. "Do you remember the Skullreaper's attack patterns?!"

Her hazel-brown eyes opened wide. Just as quickly, the light of determination filled them.

"Yes, I do," she stated.

I squeezed her shoulder again. "Good. Then you and I can deal with all the scythe attacks. If we hit them with synchronized sword skills, we should be able to neutralize their power."

She must have largely anticipated this comment already. Her face, a pale orb in the dark of night, looked more tense and resolved than before. She whispered, "But opposite the Skullreaper, the commander guarded against the other scythe all on his own."

Asuna was speaking of the Knights of the Blood's leader, Heathcliff the Holy Sword. It was because he had the greatest defense of any player in the frontline group that he was able to take on one of the scythes all on his own, helping Asuna and me last to the end. I didn't deny that fact, but if my memory was correct...

"The Skullreaper never attacked with both scythes at once. I remember that it always folded one scythe against its chest when it was about to swing the other. As long as we're watching for that, we should be capable of stopping the scythes with just the two of us."

"...All right," she said quickly. Asuna understood just as well as I did that running was not possible. Fighting was our only choice. We nodded together, then reached into our waist sacks to retrieve not healing herbs, but healing tea, and drained the bottles together. The icon for gradual HP recovery appeared, and I got to my feet.

"We're going to fight!" I shouted to the group. The others lifted themselves up from the grass. "That Life Harvester is the same as the Skullreaper boss from the seventy-fifth floor of Aincrad! Asuna and I will deal with the scythe attacks from the front! Klein, you lead the assault on the left side! Agil, you join the *Insectsite* folks on the right! Yui, use magic to attack—Misha and Kuro, protect her!"

As veterans of the Skullreaper battle, Agil and Klein replied to my rapid orders with a hearty "You got it!" They relayed orders of their own to Alice and Hyme's group, arranging formations on either side, while Yui and the two pets formed a roaming unit.

The Life Harvester came to a stop, seeming to sense our resolve. Its four eyes narrowed.

"*Jyashuuu...*," it hissed, mocking the tiny creatures that dared to challenge it.

Then it charged, racing forward with incredible speed that tore the grass under its many feet. Feeling the pressure of it bearing down on us, I shouted to Asuna, "Here we go!"

"I'm ready!"

It felt like we were back in *SAO* again. We charged, too, the gap between both sides rapidly shrinking. Once we were under thirty feet apart, the Life Harvester's right scythe tucked itself against its chest, while the left scythe pulled back sideways.

We had learned, quite painfully, that blocking the scythe with our weapons would not work. Instead, the only way to neutralize the scythe attack was for both of us to hit it with sword skills together.

This concept of "synced sword skills," which we'd developed in *SAO* and still existed among *ALO* players as a kind of unofficial practice, sounded simple—just strike the target with simultaneous sword skills—but required significant technique. The reason was that the time needed for each starting motion among the many, many sword skills was varied, as was the skill speed. So activating your skills at the same time would not make them land at the same time. And that would not produce the desired effect.

If you *could* perfectly align the moment of impact, however, the power of one plus one would instead jump to three or four. And because sword skills had a powerful knockback ability that normal attacks didn't, the two of us should be able to defend against the same scythe attack that had knocked over five people just moments earlier. It had worked against the Skullreaper, at least.

I activated the single-slice One-Handed Sword skill Vertical, and Asuna activated the single-thrust rapier skill Linear about two-tenths of a second later.

The other reason that synced sword skills were so hard was that your skill could not overlap the skill or body of your partner. If I had used Horizontal instead of Vertical, it would have hit Asuna directly on my right before it struck the Life Harvester's scythe. You had to be aware of your enemy's location, partner's location, and partner's posture, then select the best skill for the situation.

"Jyaaaaa!" the monster roared, its massive hooked scythe howling as it cut through air.

My longsword and Asuna's rapier took on different shades of blue light that split the darkness. Two edges collided with the curve of the scythe.

Kwaaannng! A tremendous crash buffeted my ears.

The staggering recoil of the sword traveled back through my right hand, elbow, and shoulder, until it burst through my spine.

But I held firm. I hadn't been tossed backward yet. The enemy's scythe didn't budge, however. It was just an infinitesimally short moment of pause. I reached for everything I could, even the Incarnation power that didn't exist in this world, searching for the strength to push the scythe back.

I felt a sudden burst in the center of my head. It almost felt like I could feel the pressure not just against my own sword, but Asuna's rapier as well. Our wills overlapped, requiring neither words nor glances to communicate.

"Ohhhh!"

"Haaaah!"

Our cries overlapping as well, we wrung out every last drop of power that our sword skills could produce.

The glowing light of our weapons flashed brighter, then went out. Our weapons were deflected, and we lost our balance.

But more importantly, the Life Harvester's left scythe was also pushed backward.

We blocked it!

Asuna and I shared this single triumphant thought in a moment of eye contact during the resulting skill delay. All we had to do was keep repeating that synchronized skill. Until our companions could work down all three HP bars.

When the delay wore off, and we could move again, the man-faced centipede was also getting back to its many feet.

This time, it folded up its left scythe and raised its right arm high. This would be a downward swing, not a sideswipe. There was no need to deflect it with sword skills, but a direct hit would be instant death, and even if you dodged it, the splash damage could cause us to fall over.

"Not yet, Kirito," Asuna murmured, staring up at the Life Harvester's scythe.

"I know," I whispered back.

The blackened tip of the scythe began to waver, trying to lure us into a stupor—and then it struck downward with blinding speed. Its target was Asuna.

"That way!" I shouted, but she was already jumping. I landed in front of her, hunching over into a defensive position to protect against the shock.

The scythe smashed into the ground with an explosive sound. The impact ripped up a wave of grass, and a shock wave rushed toward us. I felt a tremendous impact when it passed over us, but I managed to stay on my feet. There was no damage.

"Kirito, you don't need to protect me!" Asuna shouted over my shoulder.

But as I rose to my feet, I shot back, "Your leather armor can't fully protect you from that kind of area damage!"

"...That's true," she admitted with chagrin; one of Asuna's steadfast strengths was that she always admitted the truth as soon as she saw it. I was wearing Fine Steel in every piece of armor, but Asuna only had thin chest armor, arm guards, and shin guards. If she guarded adequately, she'd be able to avoid falling over, but we needed to minimize all the scratch damage, too.

The Life Harvester wrenched its scythe out of the ground with some effort; it was stuck into the soil over three feet deep. Watching carefully, I instructed, "If that downward swing attack comes again, try to get behind me!"

"Got it! Here it comes!"

The man-faced centipede pulled its newly freed arm back. It was going to swipe again.

As I prepped my sword skill, I glanced at the sides of the centipede to determine how the battle was going.

To my right, Klein's group, which included Alice and Lisbeth, was furiously attacking the over twenty legs on the creature's flank. On the left, Agil and the *Insectsite* team were busy dealing damage the same way. A number of legs had already been severed, but the Life Harvester occasionally whipped its tail spear around fiercely, causing huge damage if you didn't detect the tell and drop to the ground first. I could only trust that Klein and Agil were watching for it without fail, so I focused on the scythe again.

It was another sideswipe—except, no. The backswing was too shallow. This was...

"A feint!" Asuna cried as I turned to the right. The left scythe was already on the move. This feint motion had nearly killed me in the fight on the seventy-fifth floor. I'd been grateful to Heathcliff when he'd warned me just in time—which was ironic, because it was he, Akihiko Kayaba, who had created the Skull-reaper in the first place.

The Life Harvester quickly returned the right scythe, which it pretended to attack with, to its body, and swung the left scythe forward on a level. The path was slightly higher than the first attack. I used the diagonal Slant skill, while Asuna met it with the thrusting Streak.

Once again, I felt a moment of shared sensory information with Asuna. Our breathing aligned; we deflected the scythe again.

This was what happened against the Skullreaper, too. We shared thoughts without using words and maintained perfect synchronization without a single mistake. Much time had passed since that fight—we were in a different world, with different weapons and different stats—but the link that connected us was still alive. We could surely win this fight, as we won before.

On the right, Kirito!

Let's block it here!

We aligned ourselves with communication so smooth that I couldn't even tell if it was spoken or psychic. With each successful counter, the distractions faded away. The fear that even a single failure would lead to our deaths evaporated, as did the impatience of wondering how long we'd have to do this in order to win—leaving only one sensation: the pleasure of becoming one with Asuna, optimizing our movements into the ideal.

And it was this trance state that swept our feet out from under us at the very last moment.

"Shagyuooooooo!!"

I couldn't count how many times the beast had roared by now. The Life Harvester retracted both scythes as far as they could go along the ground. That was a motion we had never seen before, even back in *SAO*.

If Asuna and I were in a normal state, we would have detected that an unknown attack was coming and attempted to retreat outside of the scythes' swing range.

But having countered so many attacks in a row in an almost-automatic state, it took an extra half a second to snap out of the trance state and regain my usual decision-making ability.

The withdrawn scythes began to issue a crimson glow. This was a special attack the Skullreaper didn't have. There was no time to evade, and there was no way that Asuna and I could each block a scythe that was boosted with extra power.

"Kirito—," Asuna rasped at the same time that the screams of our companions filled the air.

We'd just have to hit the ground and pray—but no, I had a better option.

"Forward!!" I shouted, pushing her from behind. We leaped forward together.

Burning red scythes rushed toward us from the left and right. I could feel the premonition of fatal damage prickling on my skin as I raced for all I was worth.

The Life Harvester's forelegs were about ten feet of upper arms, attached to fifteen feet of giant scythes. When swinging just one scythe, it pulled the other against its chest to keep from smashing them together. Now it was swinging both of them, however. While the blades themselves were thin enough that they could cross each other without touching, the thick arms would collide. That should leave a narrow gap, right in front of its body.

If it didn't, Asuna and I were going to die.

The blades rushed inward. I could hear the *kshaa!* of the two scythes scraping against each other already behind us. Before us was the massive body, covered in blue-black carapace. With the Skullreaper, there had been enough of a gap to slip underneath the body if necessary, but the Life Harvester's loins featured four protuberances like spikes that blocked any gap.

"Right up against it!" I cried, leaping to the side of one of the spikes. Asuna did the same, pressing against me. The scythes continued to rush toward us from behind…

Clank! They met dully.

I turned around to see the joint areas of both forelegs, smashed together and locking the two of us inside a small triangle of space.

"*Jyaaaaa!!*" it roared with fury. I looked up to see it glaring down at us, freakish mouth opened as far as it could go. The HP readout over its head was down to the final bar, with barely 20 percent left. Our companions had been faithfully grinding down its HP. We had to finish this encounter strong, so that their efforts paid off.

"*Jyashuuuu!!*" it hissed again. The Life Harvester's foreleg joints clacked as they collided, again and again. Its mouth opened and closed furiously above our heads. But the monster's thick armor narrowed its range of motion, so that it couldn't do anything while we clung to its torso. If it started charging forward, we'd have to move as well, but it seemed to be having enough trouble just staying upright; the others must have removed most of its legs by now.

"This is our chance, Kirito!" Asuna cried, readying her rapier. Sensing her plan, I lifted my longsword to my right shoulder.

"*Jyaaaaa!!*" it roared for the third time.

My jumping skill Sonic Leap and Asuna's charging skill Shooting Star activated, aimed directly upward—and aided by the boost of leaping. The combination of avatar jump strength and system assistance carried us upward with momentum that would be impossible in real life.

Longsword and rapier, trailing two colors of light, burst through the huge open mouth, and its jaw opened up, down, left, and right.

The pale flash bulged, extending into a pillar of light that passed through the inside of its four eyes. Light also shone from cracks in the shell and joints, then pulsed—and exploded.

The Life Harvester writhed backward, spraying pale flames from its head. We jumped away from the creature, doing backflips in the air. Once we'd landed, I checked the HP bar: just under 10 percent left.

Sensing that we could finish it off with an all-out assault, I breathed in to give the order to the group.

But before I could, the Life Harvester bellowed with more rage than any it had expressed to this point.

"Jyaggrrraaaaaaahh!!"

Filthy red flames rose in the four damaged eye sockets after our attack damage faded. The massive body trembled and shuddered, trapped in place with over 80 percent of its legs lost. The spear on its tail smacked the ground a few times. It looked like the warning signs of a frantic state, when a nearly dead boss tossed out its usual attack patterns for one final burst of desperate thrashing.

If everyone here committed to a total offensive plan with no thought for defense, we could probably grind out the last few percent of its HP bar. But if even a tiny bit was still left at the end, its counterattack could possibly wipe us all out. Should we pull back for a little distance and take our time with a safer strategy?

There was no guarantee that Asuna and I could avoid that previous double-scythe attack again, however. Our strategy had worked specifically *because* the two of us were keeping the Life Harvester entirely occupied. If it turned its attention on the people around its flanks, it might cause our formation to crumble.

After coming so far, are we stuck without a winning option? I lamented.

"ℵℵℵℵℵ!"

A familiar screeching voice issued from the forest to the west of the battlefield.

From among the trees leaped a number of figures, much smaller than a human. But this was not some new group of monsters. It was the rodent-type humanoid NPCs we'd left behind in Ruis na Ríg, the Patter. There were ten of them in total. Each one held an iron pitchfork in its left hand and a crude spear whittled from wood in its right.

The one in the lead, whom I took to be female, shouted again. "ℵℵℵ!!"

On that cue, the ten of them released their wooden spears as one. The projectiles flew with unimaginable force from such small bodies and struck the Life Harvester's head one after the other. Half just bounced off the carapace, but the others sank into muscle, taking down another 3 percent. Just 5 percent left.

"Jyaaaa!"

The Life Harvester roared and stuck its few remaining legs into the ground, managing to turn its body. It was clearly targeting the Patter now. But the small mice men gripped their pitchforks with both hands and stood firm.

Then a new voice entered the fray. "ℵℵℵℵℵℵ!!"

More silhouettes were rushing out of the woods now. This time they were human—but not players. It was the other NPC group that had moved into Ruis na Ríg, the Bashin tribespeople. When their leader, the stout warrior Yzelma, saw me, she shouted, "ℵℵℵ!"

I didn't have the skills for either the Patter or the Bashin language, but I understood instinctually what she had said. It was some form of "Are you afraid or something?" or "Let's do this!"

Withdrawal was no longer an option. We would press a total offensive assault, and we would either emerge victorious or perish as a group.

Drawing a breath and holding it in my gut, I raised my sword and yelled, "All-out attack!!"

The roars of my companions matched the roar of the Life Harvester.

2

"...So I guess insect people eat the same things we do..."

I replied to Leafa's whisper with a quick, surreptitious nod.

We were seated in a giant circle of over sixty people—players and NPCs—in the empty space bordering the pet stables in the northern part of Ruis na Ríg. The fan-shaped empty lot was planned to be a large farm in the future, measuring thirty yards side to side and fifteen yards front to back, so we still had plenty of room, but even still, the sight of all the former *ALO* players (plus one from *GGO*), the former *Insectsite* players, the Bashin, and the Patter all mingled together around a roaring bonfire was truly something to behold.

The *Insectsite* players, in particular, had not been anthropomorphized much, if at all; their faces were still those of grasshoppers and mantises and stag beetles, which made them rather frightening to look at. Despite the fact that they should realistically be licking tree sap and eating plants, those grotesque jaws were busy chowing down on fresh-cooked meat, which looked like something out of a horror movie.

"I wonder what the inside of their mouths are like," muttered Alice, who was seated on my left.

To Leafa's right, Agil was drinking something resembling beer.

He replied, "I could see it during battle. They looked just like human mouths inside."

Alice made a rather strange face, and I couldn't help but grunt, "Freaky!"

That was probably because creating an oral structure that was too different from reality would be difficult for a player to process. Back in *ALO*, I once transformed into a demon with an elongated, wolflike muzzle and tried to eat another player, and I could remember how difficult it was to actually get them into my mouth.

Fortunately, there were no children crying at the sight of a giant grasshopper chomping on meat. It was currently 9:20 PM on September 30th, so the five Patter children were asleep in their dwellings in the east area of town, and the ten Bashin who had moved here were all adults.

But if Yui's conjecture that NPCs in the world of *Unital Ring* were adjusted to match the capacity of their dwellings was accurate, the Bashin might soon have children of their own. The problem was that this place was going to be a battlefield tomorrow night, so I hoped they could put off their childbirth until later. We had to concoct a plan to evacuate the Patter children if necessary. The more time went on, the more I needed those Bashin and Patter language skills...

Just then, Yzelma the Bashin chief came striding over to me, holding a massive platter in both hands. She had been drinking heavily, a cheerful smile plastered on her reddened face. She slammed the plate down in front of me, sat, and belted out "אא!"— not that I knew what that meant.

There was a sizzling, thick-cut steak on her platter, which was at least two and a half feet in diameter. It was a simple dish, just a huge chunk of meat that had been seared over the fire, but it had a mysterious new seasoned smell, the likes of which I hadn't experienced in this world before, probably due to some Bashin spices she'd brought from home.

"אא!" she bellowed again, motioning with the plate. I decided that she was telling me to eat, so I stabbed the steak with my wooden fork. I lifted the cut of meat, a foot long and an inch thick; globs of fat and juices dripped off it.

It looked and smelled delicious—but there was a mental hurdle that kept me from chomping down on it: in a word, because it was the flesh of the gigantic man-faced centipede field boss, the Life Harvester.

Just thirty minutes earlier, we were launching into an all-out raid on the Life Harvester as it went into a frenzied state. The beast had lifted its twin scythes and tail spear high as dozens of sword skills flashed around it. The key that overwrote the possibility of a party-destroying counterattack was my jumping three-part Sharp Nail skill. The third hit split the Life Harvester's solar plexus, and when its third and final HP bar disappeared, the adrenaline was so intense that I could have set off the Amu-Sphere's safety shutoff.

As befitting an ultra-tough enemy, the Life Harvester dropped a ton of experience and items, but the most numerous of those were meat, shell, and bone. There was so much meat, in fact, that we couldn't carry it all, even after stuffing everyone's capacity full. It was Yzelma's suggestion of a celebratory feast that finally gave us something to *do* with all that meat.

The Bashin grabbed the piles of meat stacked by the bonfire and sliced them up, skewered them, and spiced them before roasting. The *Insectsite* players, the Patter, and Klein were all delighted to chow down, but I found it difficult not to recall the grotesque image of the Life Harvester, and I was hoping to pass on it—or at least wait to try the stew that Asuna and Yui were using their Cooking skill to flavor—when Yzelma came over.

I glanced to my right, but Leafa looked away. I turned to the left, and Alice averted her eyes. The only person who would face me was Yzelma, directly in front of me. She beamed. There was no escape.

The Life Harvester had a centipede-like design, but to be a true insect, it would need to have a boneless, monocoque structure. So if it had a skeletal structure inside of flesh, that made it a vertebrate animal, closer in biological terms to a cow than a bug.

Or so I told myself, carefully ignoring the knowledge that there were no vertebrates with more than four legs. I took a big bite of the thick steak.

Despite the charred burns on the surface, the inside was appropriately soft. It seemed a bit closer to mutton than beef in flavor, but the Bashin spices made the gamey part of the meat more fragrant. In all honesty, it tasted a rank or two above the thornspike cave bear and Giyoru bison meat—as long as you didn't let the horrid visage of the Life Harvester cross your mind.

I chewed the meat until it vanished into the void within my avatar and shouted, "It's good!"

But Yzelma just looked stunned, so I looked to my companions for help. "Um, what's the Bashin word for *delicious*?"

Leafa and Alice seemed confused by the question. Silica, who was feeding Pina nuts nearby, glanced over and said, "It's *jeemeh*."

Setting aside the question of how she had learned Bashin, I turned to Yzelma and said, "Jeemeh!"

The warrior's expression did not change.

"Jeemeh! This is super jeemeh! Crazy jeemeh!"

The other girls couldn't hold back their giggles. I kept repeating the word—*jeemeh, jeemeh*—changing the intonation slightly each time, until around the tenth attempt, when Yzelma's broad face broke into a smile.

"אא! Jeemeh!"

She pounded my right shoulder with a powerful hand and distributed more steaks from the platter to Leafa, then Agil and his friends, and returned to the fire. A familiar message window appeared over the sight of her retreating back.

Bashin skill gained. Proficiency has risen to 1.

Once the window disappeared, I asked Silica, "About how high do you have to get your language skill proficiency before you can use it?"

"Hmmm. To be able to hold even the most basic kind of communication, you'll need a proficiency of around ten. I'm still only at fifteen, so I can't act like much of an expert, though..."

"Ten…," I repeated, thinking it wouldn't actually be that bad.

Then Silica grinned and added, "By the way, to get to ten, you only need to master about thirty words. Good luck!"

"…Ah…I see…"

So if I wanted to get both Bashin and Patter language skills up to a proficiency of 10, I'd need to memorize and perfectly pronounce sixty vocabulary words that would have zero use in the real world. And I'm sure that the effort would squeeze at least two or three English words out of my brain in exchange.

I have no idea who created this game, but I have to wonder why they made it so damn complicated, I swore to myself, taking another big bite of Life Harvester meat, which I chose to shorten to "harve."

Every single person at the feast ate until they were full to bursting, but we didn't consume even 10 percent of the total weight of Life Harvester meat we'd received.

If this were the Underworld, the life of the meat would run out very quickly if the remainder wasn't dried or frozen or salted, but fortunately, the durability of materials did not decrease in *Unital Ring*, as long as they were stored in your inventory. In other words, for the moment, we'd solved the issue of Ruis na Ríg's burgeoning population's food needs. Eating steak for every meal was going to get boring, but Asuna and Yui's herbal stew was delicious and a bit gentler in flavor, and there would be plenty of other ways to cook it. On top of that, Misha the bear, Kuro the panther, and Asuna's pet lizard, Aga, all seemed to love their new harve diet.

The feast lasted until ten at night, when the Patter and the Bashin returned to their dwellings. That left our group and the twenty former *Insectsite* players in the empty lot by the stable. We took the opportunity to introduce ourselves once again.

The leader of the insects was Agil's wife, Hyme the orchid mantis. Her senior officers were Zarion the Actaeon rhinoceros beetle and Beeming the *Cantharolethrus steinheili* stag beetle. After the handshakes concluded, I finally got around to asking the question I'd been wondering about Argo the Rat.

"So...Argo, why were you with them?"

The diminutive info dealer drained the mug of beer in her hand before answering, "Welp, I said I'd do everything I could last night, didn't I?"

"Yeah, you did say that."

"Truth is: I've known Hyme for a little while..."

"Oh...from Agil's route?" I asked, then realized that couldn't be correct. Argo showed up just two days ago, and she'd been effectively missing before then. If she had been in contact with Agil, he wouldn't have been so shocked when I introduced her last night.

"Nope. Different route," Argo replied, as I suspected she would. She glanced at the insects. "I've been researchin' the globalization of the Seed Nexus for the past year or so. *Insectsite*'s one o' the bigger Seed games in America, but almost no one in Japan plays it...So when I finally found someone who was, it turned out to be Hyme."

"Whoa...It's that big in America?" I asked, more than a little stunned by the revelation.

It wasn't Argo who replied, however, but Asuna: "Yes, I was only aware of the name of the game because of Yuuki. She said the Sleeping Knights played it for just a little bit before they came to *ALO*."

"Ohhh..."

Even though I hadn't been as close with Yuuki the Absolute Sword, I still felt my chest tighten at the mention of her name. Asuna was smiling, but I couldn't help but see the light in her eyes wavering.

I reached out without thinking and brushed Asuna's hand before looking back to Argo. "All right, I know how *you* know Hyme... but why were you being chased by the Life Harvester with them?"

"Well, ah..."

Argo glanced around, then picked up a long stick off the ground. She used it to draw a circle in the dirt about three feet across.

"It's probably more complicated than this, but let's just assume this is the *Unital Ring* world map, m'kay?"

"Got it." We nodded. Sinon, Alice, and several of the *Insectsite* players came over to surround the map.

Unbothered, Argo continued her explanation. "If north is this way, then where we are is right about here." She jabbed the end of the stick at a spot in the southwest part of the map, quite close to the edge, in fact.

"How do you know we're there?" Sinon asked.

Argo flipped the branch upward and pointed at the night sky, where trails of rain clouds still remained. "You remember the direction the aurora ran on the first night, Sinocchi?"

Apparently, Argo was content to continue the pattern that began with Alice as Alicchi. Sinon blinked twice with surprise, then bobbed her shoulders. "Yes, I think it was northeast."

"Meanin' in this direction." Argo pointed the branch toward the Ruis na Ríg spot again but stopped herself. "Or was it a little more north than that?"

"Huh? Oh…yeah, I guess," Sinon agreed. She crouched down and poked a new hole in the dirt with her finger, a few inches northwest of Ruis na Ríg. "There was an aurora in the sky, and when I heard the announcement, I was on the other side of the Giyoru Savanna…around here, I think. If I'm right about what you're saying, Argo, the aurora I saw would have been pointing a slightly different direction than the one Kirito saw."

She drew a line to the northeast from her point—toward the center of the circular map. Argo grinned at her and drew a line to the same point from Ruis na Ríg. It also went toward the center, which would mean that, as Sinon had said, they were at slightly different angles.

"Meaning," rumbled Agil, who had joined the circle at some point. He turned to the praying mantis avatar standing next to him and asked in English, "Hyme, which direction did the aurora flow for you?"

Hyme's razor-like jaw moved, emitting a smooth, mature woman's voice. "Almost exactly north."

She extended her right arm, using the point on the end to draw a line directly north, about four inches west from Ruis na Ríg's location. Based on the three lines on the map, Argo's point was clear.

"You're saying that the aurora appeared all over *Unital Ring*'s world in a big…radial pattern…?" I murmured.

Argo nodded and drew a few more lines from the east and north side of the map toward the center. "That's exactly it. Gatherin' info on the net, I found stories of the aurora travelin' west—and south, too. I'm guessing that all the Seed game players who got converted into *UR* were placed in a big ring along the outer edge of the map. And from there, it was *On your mark, get set…*"

Alice picked up where Argo left off. "Aim for the land revealed by the heavenly light, in the center of the world. In that sense, it was good fortune that Sinon's *GGO* players were placed right next to the *ALO* players…"

"I wouldn't say we were *right* next to each other," Sinon remarked dryly. The others who made the journey to the Giyoru Savanna nodded. As a matter of fact, the wall dungeon where they met Sinon was in the middle of the savanna, and that was already nearly twenty miles from Ruis na Ríg. Sinon had apparently traveled about the same distance before she met up with us, so that meant the ruins for the *GGO* players were close to forty miles away—farther than the distance between the sylph city of Swilvane and the World Tree at the center of Alfheim.

Leafa was picking up on the same thing. She stared at the map on the ground and murmured, "Argo, just how long is the radius of this world…?"

"Hmmmm," Argo grunted. She used the tip of the stick to tap three points: the *GGO* players' starting point, Ruis na Ríg, and the *Insectsite* players' starting point. "I only drew these three spots based on a hunch, y'see. But if the scale here is accurate, the distance from these points to the center of the map would be… somewhere between three hundred seventy-five and four hundred twenty-five miles?"

"Four hundred?!" Leafa shrieked. Lisbeth and Silica groaned

"Oh nooo…," and I could even hear, belatedly, the English-speaking insects exclaiming *"No way!"* and *"Are you kidding me?!"*

I couldn't blame them. If that was just the radius, that meant the diameter was twice that length—over 850 miles. Alfheim alone had a diameter of sixty miles, and that felt nearly endless. Even locked in the death game of *SAO*, a single floor of Aincrad being six miles across seemed utterly huge. Eight hundred miles was simply impossible to understand. It was nearly the length from Hokkaido in the north down to Kyushu in the southwest. And in terms of the Underworld…

"……!"

Suddenly, I bolted upright, my body trembling.

I looked up and met eyes with Alice, who was directly across from me. The cat-eared knight's blue eyes were just as wide as mine.

I had a feeling she had come to the same conclusion: What if Argo's rough estimate was just slightly larger? Say, a radius of 450 miles instead of four hundred…

Then it would perfectly match the radius of the human realm that was surrounded by the End Mountains.

But even if the numbers do match, that's just a coincidence, I thought, which Alice seemed to sense. She nodded silently.

Aside from the use of the Seed package, there was no connection between the Underworld and *Unital Ring*. And the Underworld wasn't connected to the Seed Nexus, which made any possibility of a link exceedingly remote. It was better to focus on the situation around us, rather than trying to look for meaning in coincidences, I told myself.

The murmuring of the group around me died down, too. I cleared my throat and got back to the original topic. "So we have a broad understanding of the structure of the world map. But how does that connect to the reason you were together with Hyme's group?"

"Oh yeah! I was explaining that, wasn't I?" Argo joked. She shot a glance at the line of insect soldiers before continuing, "It's simple, really. Ever since this whole thing started, I've been get-tin' feedback from Hyme about their situation. The *Insectsite* folks said things were real fishy with them, so they asked if I wanted to help 'em out."

"Fishy...?" I repeated.

From ahead and on my left, someone said, "Kiri, how much do you know about *Insectsite*?"

It was coming from the praying mantis with a white exterior and pink highlights: Hyme. I was taken aback by her fluent Japanese and nickname for me. I shook my head and mumbled, "Um...h-hardly anything..."

"That's natural. In *Insectsite*, players are all arthropods, and there's a faction war happening between hexapods—six-legged insects—and others like Chelicerata and myriapods. Chelicerata include spiders and scorpions, while myriapods are centipedes and millipedes and the like."

"...Wouldn't most players side with the insects?" I asked.

The mantis's triangular head bobbed. "Ex-zactly. The Chelic-erata and myriapods—based on the number of legs, we call them Eight-or-Mores, or more commonly, Eighmores—have always been overwhelmed by the insect side—and consistently losing territory. So there's been some rebalancing lately, so that Eigh-mores have way stronger stats and skills now. The Eighmores were starting a furious counterattack to tilt the scales when this whole incident happened."

"So, um...I'm guessing that the *Insectsite* players showed up in the same place, both insects and Eighmores?"

"Yeah."

"Wouldn't that lead to absolute chaos?"

"It did," Hyme confirmed. Zarion and Beeming, who were receiving interpretation from Agil, snarled in their own lan-guage. Once they were done expressing their frustration, Hyme resumed her story.

"With the first few hours of being forced to convert to this game, nearly all the Sixes—that's us, the insects—were killed by

Eighmores. It was inside the grace period, so we revived, but we lost all our inherited equipment to them and had no way to come back from behind. Most of the Sixes didn't leave the starting ruins regardless, but our troop had a feeling that the grace period was going to end, and we escaped."

"Troop…? Is that what they call guilds in your game?"

"Yeah…In fact, we were one of the top-ten troops in *Insectsite*. But it was really hard to advance without gear, and the grace period ended at some point, plus the Eighmores started rushing out of the ruins to chase us down. There was no way out for us… How do you say that in Japanese, again?"

"Um…we'd say *nicchi mo sacchi mo ikanai*, I suppose…"

"Okay, so we were all *nicchi-sacchi*, and that's when I got the message from Argo."

I exhaled, relieved to see where the story was going at last.

The bonfire in the center of the clearing was nearly dead now, just the last little flickers of flames remaining, around which Misha, Kuro, and Aga slept soundly. And now that I looked closer, even Pina had left Silica's head to curl up atop Kuro's back. While Aga hadn't taken part in the battle, a worse outcome against the Life Harvester could have spelled disaster for Misha or Kuro—or perhaps both of them.

Each of these pets had been tamed through a confluence of circumstances, but even in the few days we'd had them, I had to admit that I was surprisingly attached. I didn't want to imagine losing them, but that just meant I needed to think long and hard about how to use them in battle to minimize risk.

I turned away from the animals to Argo again. "So today, you were traveling to the *Insectsite* area to meet up with Hyme and her friends. If you'd just said the word, we could have sent someone with you…"

"Nah, I was hiding and sneaking past all the monsters along the way. Safer for me to go alone."

"Oh yeah, hide-and-seek master?" I needled good-naturedly. "How'd you end up getting chased by that huge monster, then?"

The Rat made a bitter face. While she'd traveled to meet them alone, she was returning in a huge party of twenty-one, so that was an unfair question. I felt a bit bad about asking it.

"That was my mistake," she admitted.

"Wait...really?"

"The info agent part o' me got greedy. Listen, Kiri-boy, *Unital Ring*'s got some unnatural features."

"Oh...?"

Asuna and the other girls leaned in closer with interest. The center of attention again, Argo resumed poking at the map with her stick.

To the southwest of Ruis na Ríg's dot, in the lower right of Giyoru Savanna, she drew a small circle, rather than a dot. Then she added another, far to the northwest.

"Here and there around the world, there are perfectly circular basins. At the biggest, they're about six miles across, and even the smaller ones are still two or three miles. The forests and rivers are all perfectly natural in design, so you gotta figure there's a particular reason these basins are so circular, huh?" she stated. I murmured and stared, lost in thought.

"Oh...That's the basin where the Bashin village is!" Lisbeth cried, pointing at the circle closer to Ruis na Ríg. And Sinon indicated the circle farther away. "I suspect this basin is where the Ornith village is. I just assumed that they had dug the land down that way...But I suppose it was a natural feature instead."

Asuna and Silica nodded along with them, but I had seen neither basin for myself. Yui was examining the map closely next to Asuna. She had visited the Bashin village twice, so I asked her, "Yui, was the basin where the Bashin live really that circular?"

"I did not have the opportunity to view it from a high altitude, so I have not confirmed the full scale of it...But from what I observed, the arc of the basin's boundary has an estimated roundness deviation of about two inches. That number is certainly impossible to imagine coming from the Seed program's landscape-generation process..."

It took me a moment to digest this explanation. A roundness deviation of two inches meant that the miles-wide basin, when measured against a perfect geometric circle of the same size, wouldn't deviate more than two inches from its border. Indeed, that could only mean it was intentionally placed by the world's creator.

"...What are these circular basins for anyway?" I asked Argo.

The info dealer's grimace was clearly visible under her hood. "That's what I'm lookin' up. For now, I know there's been over thirty of these basins found all over the map. And there's somethin' inside every one of 'em. NPC villages, ruins, dungeons...I spotted one of them around here after meeting up with Hyme tonight, in fact."

She drew a third circle on the map, two inches east from Ruis na Ríg—which was probably more like twenty miles in actual distance.

"There's no intel about this one on the net yet, so I wanted to at least see what was inside it. I asked them to wait outside, and I snuck in. Inside a forest of dead trees, there was a stone circle ruin, and I felt sure I smelled treasure inside. That was when that huge freakin' humantipede jumped out at me..."

"...I see."

Over to the east of the clearing, the only sight were the trees of the Great Zelletelio Forest that surrounded Ruis na Ríg. But of course, the map continued on beyond the boundary of the forest, which was only a tiny part of the world of *Unital Ring*.

"And you got chased by the Life Harvester from that basin all the way to where you met up with us."

"Who would have guessed the thing would give chase for twenty whole miles? I really screwed things up for Hyme's group...," Argo lamented, a rare sign of deflation from her.

But Zarion, the something-or-other rhinoceros beetle, said happily, *"Never mind that, girl! I had a blast!"*

Beeming, the something-or-other stag beetle, added, *"I felt so much better after we beat that guy!"*

The other insects chipped in with their own words of reassurance. To my surprise, Argo replied with English just as smooth as Agil's.

"Hey, do you think the reason that giant freak chased us so long is because it was an Eighmore, and y'all are Sixes?"

The insects erupted in laughter, and I couldn't help but think, *Wow, Argo, this is incredible!*

With the situation fully explained now, I had no reservations about bringing the twenty insects into Ruis na Ríg. If anything, I was ready to beg them to join us...except that there was one warning to give them before that could happen.

Employing plenty of help from Agil, I used every last bit of my English ability in explaining to Hyme and her friends the ultimate danger that was approaching us as soon as tomorrow night.

Upon learning about the witch Mutasina, leader of the Virtual Study Society, and her terrifying suffocation magic, plus the army of over a hundred players under her thrall coming to attack our town, Hyme engaged in a very serious conversation with her companions.

She turned back to me at one point to ask, "Is there any possibility of cooperation with this Mutasina?"

"......"

I couldn't give her an immediate answer. Without realizing it, I lifted my hand to touch the throat guard of my armor. Beneath it, there was a stark, ringed black symbol around my neck, symbol of Mutasina's suffocation magic. In the Stiss Ruins far to the south, Mutasina could thump the butt of her staff against the ground, and I would be reduced to rolling around on the ground, unable to breathe.

There was no doubt that her overall power was in the top echelon of the entire *Unital Ring*. If we could work alongside her, we would have a tremendously reassuring ally. *If.*

Picking my English words carefully, I translated Mutasina's words for them to hear.

You might cooperate now, but the closer the goal becomes, the more our teams will compete with one another. In the end, even the players within a team will fight and kill one another. But as long as my magic is active upon you, we can avoid that situation. Do you see? This is the best and most effective means of getting to the finish line, isn't it?

Even after the final question at the end had been relayed, the insects did not speak for some time. I started to worry that my choice of English had been poor, until Hyme spat, *"Ridiculous."*

She crossed her thorny arms before her chest and said in Japanese, "No, I don't think we'll be making friends with her. And now that I've heard about this, I can't possibly move on and pretend it didn't happen."

"W…well, I want you to consider this carefully. We're talking about an army of a hundred…You could stay here for the night and leave tomorrow morning, and no one will think the worse of you."

"Yes, a hundred players is no laughing matter. But between your friends, Kiri, those cool natives, the cute mice, and all of us, that makes sixty, right? I *know* we're better in terms of individual combat ability, and we've got the advantage of our defenses. It'd be closer than you think, wouldn't it?"

"Well…that's true."

It seemed like desperate odds for us this morning, but the twenty insects added to the equation made for a much different picture. And the players on Mutasina's side had no idea that we had the *Insectsite* team on our side, so if they took part in the big battle, the visual shock of those grotesque insect avatars might have a psychological effect on the enemy. As long as we cooked up a good plan and confused them with traps and sneak attacks, we might have a chance to win.

But…

"A good chance" wasn't good enough. Fighting off an enemy invasion only to lose half of our number wasn't really victory. If you died at all in *Unital Ring*, you could never log back in. I didn't want to lose a single companion until we could beat it altogether.

And it was doubly true for NPCs, who really would die for good. I only wanted to fight if I was certain that we could turn back a hundred enemies without a single casualty on our side. And those players in Mutasina's army were under her coercion, so I didn't really want to cause mass casualties among them, either.

"...If we can just do something about Mutasina before the battle begins," I proposed, as I'd done in the meeting before we fought the Life Harvester.

Klein, who'd been through somewhere between ten and twenty beers, lamented, "That's what it comes to, huh? It ain't in my playbook to do a sneak attack on a lady I've never even seen before, but if they're gonna attack us, I guess it's gotta be done..."

"If you want to go alone and talk her out of it, be our guest," Lisbeth suggested.

He shook his head and wailed, "Hell no! Not if it means walking right up to her and having her cast that choking magic on me!" Our friends and even the insects chuckled at this.

To my right, I could feel Argo's gaze on me, and I carefully avoided looking back at her.

Last night, when traveling to the Stiss Ruins where the *ALO* players started, I fell under the effects of Mutasina's choking magic, the Noose of the Accursed—but I hadn't told my friends yet. The only person who knew, because she'd been there, was Argo.

I made her promise to stay quiet; because if the others knew, they would demand to place solving my curse at the top of the priority list when we had a mountain of other tasks to stay on top of. I didn't want to be the reason we were falling behind on leveling up and getting better gear.

At every opportunity, Argo sent me telepathic messages saying "*Ya better tell 'em*," but once the Siege of Ruis na Ríg began— or Defense of Ruis na Ríg, from our perspective—Mutasina wouldn't activate the Noose spell. Not only would it immobilize me, it would affect all one hundred of her followers as well.

My guess—which was almost certainly accurate—was that

killing Mutasina or destroying her staff would undo the Noose. I could explain the situation to Asuna and everyone else *after* that point and apologize for keeping it secret, I told myself, to assuage my feeling of guilt.

I turned to Hyme. "I'd be very grateful if you stayed around to fight. If so, I think that it will be the key to our victory, as you said. But at the current moment, it will be hard for us to fight off a hundred enemies without losing anyone. So I want to search for a way to avoid this war, until the last possible moment, and if it comes to this…I think we should consider abandoning the town."

No one spoke for a long time.

Now that the Patter and the Bashin were here, with the Patter having had children to boot, we had just come to the conclusion hours ago that we could not abandon the town. The others had to be wondering what I was thinking to go back to it again.

But after experiencing the possibility of total loss against the Life Harvester, the chill running down my spine was still present. I didn't want to lose my companions. I didn't want anyone to die. I would be happier to just stop playing *Unital Ring* if going on meant losing anyone…

I clenched my fists briefly, then turned to look Asuna in the face. Her eyes, which smoldered with quiet flames, stared right back into mine. It seemed to me, however, that there was a faint note of misgiving in them, too.

I couldn't blame her. The center of Ruis na Ríg was our home, the log cabin. It should have been smashed to pieces along with the twenty-second floor of New Aincrad when it fell, but through a number of miracles and an incredible amount of effort, we managed to make it land in this forest. Abandoning Ruis na Ríg meant abandoning our home.

Amid the heavy silence, a voice arrived that was as cool and refreshing as a night breeze.

"Kirito, if you think only of what happens in defeat before you fight, you will end up losing winnable battles," said Alice. Her back was proud and straight, and her hand rested on the pommel of the sword on her left hip. Even wearing crude iron armor, she looked just like the Integrity Knight she had been in her old glory days. But what was I saying? She was still the proud and noble Osmanthus Knight, of course.

"Of course, it is important to consider all circumstances," she continued, "but they must be considered for the sake of victory; is that not true? I believe that it would be losing sight of the entire purpose if we were to choose to run in order to avoid battle."

I couldn't argue with that.

During the Otherworld War that took place in the Underworld, Alice threw herself into a battle that was three thousand against fifty thousand, and against those astronomical odds, she led her troops to victory with a massive sacred art of her own making. At the time, I was in a comatose state, so I wasn't able to help—and those words coming from her now were a sucker punch directly to my heart.

Yes…we had over twenty hours before Mutasina's army attacked. It was too early to be giving up yet. If we thought hard, we might find a way—a way to defeat a raid party of a hundred without losing a single one of our friends.

In the corner of my view, it said *ten pm*. The evening was getting long by now, but for VRMMO players, this was prime time. Perhaps now was a good point to move to the log cabin and start strategic planning for real.

But Hyme, who'd been discussing something with her companions, turned to me and motioned nimbly with her strange praying mantis shoulders. "Kiri, I hate to say it, but my friends need to log out now."

"Huh? Oh…right, the others are diving from America, huh…?"

Agil's wife lived in Tokyo, but the other nineteen of them lived in the United States, I presumed, so the time difference was a consideration. I tried to calculate what time it would be over there. Yui was thoughtful enough to recognize the look of pain on my face and did it for me.

"It is currently five AM on the West Coast, and eight AM on the East Coast!"

"Thanks, Yui. Yeah, that's a long night…Sorry for taking so much of your time," I said.

Hyme's triangular head shook from side to side. "No, we had a great time. Do you mind if they use those shacks to log out?" she asked, pointing at the stables on the north end of the clearing.

They might have been nonhuman avatars, but it didn't feel right to treat them like stable animals. Instead, I guided them to the inn—which wasn't yet functioning as a business—on the south side, where Zarion and the others could log off.

Left behind on her own, Hyme came to the cabin with us. We sat on the floor of the spacious living room to resume our talk.

On a bulletin board I built using the Beginner Carpentry skill, I drew a simple map of the environs around Ruis na Ríg using some bonfire ash. Then I posed a question to the group. "Think about this as if you were Mutasina. If you were going to attack this town with a hundred players, what strategy would you use?"

They were taken aback by the sudden mental exercise but took the scenario seriously.

Ruis na Ríg was a circle two hundred feet across, surrounded by sturdy ten-foot-tall stone walls and wooden gates in the four ordinal directions: northeast, southeast, southwest, and northwest. Thick forest surrounded the town, with the only exception being a road from the southwest gate leading to the Maruba River that ran to the west of the forest.

After thirty seconds, the first to speak was Agil, who'd been freed from his interpreting duties now that the Americans were gone. "From what you've said, it sounds like this Mutasina has a real sick personality, so I doubt her forces will just come rushing right up the southwest road."

"I agree," said Silica, Pina resting on her head. Misha, Aga, and Kuro were sleeping in the stable, but Pina's default location in this world was its owner's head. "Mutasina will want to minimize the loss of her allies, too, so I think she'll try to come up with a plan that will catch us by surprise. Like, hiding separate parties in the woods on either side of the road, then catching us in a pincer attack when we rush out at them…"

The rest of the party murmured in agreement. Luring enemies out of their safe zone into being surrounded was a classic strategy against monsters. If it worked in a PvP setting, it would have great effect, too.

"I wonder if clearing out the surrounding forest is the safest thing to do, in the end…," Sinon questioned. Again, murmurs arose, sounding more conflicted this time.

Argo, who was sitting cross-legged against the wall, rocked back and forth. "I ain't just sayin' this because I'm using a scouting build, but you can use forests in a big free-for-all, too. Clearing out the trees to open up the land removes the danger of an ambush, but it also leaves us with fewer options for strategy."

"Indeed," agreed Asuna. "The reason Schulz's ambush group burned the forest first was probably for light—and also to protect against us launching a sneak attack through the trees. I would guess that, generally speaking, in the open the advantage will go to the side with numbers…"

"That's true," said Sinon, who did not have a rebuttal.

The next to speak was Yui, who usually dedicated herself to listening carefully in discussions like these. "In that case, would Mutasina attempt to level the forest before launching her attack? You would need some heavy machinery in the real world, but in *Unital Ring*, depending on your skill level and tools, you can cut down a grown spiral pine in about ten seconds. With a hundred players, I think they could clear out every last tree within five hundred yards of Ruis na Ríg in an hour."

"……Uh-huh…" In the back of my mind, I thought of the witch as I had witnessed her at the Stiss Ruins. "There's no way that the Noose of the Accursed is the only spell that Mutasina can use. If she can use other attack spells, she'll want to remove any cover to hide behind…So it seems possible that she'll open up the land around us, then put another tactic into play."

"Great thinking, Yui! It's so good to have you with us!" exclaimed Lisbeth, hugging the girl and scrunching her hair.

Asuna watched this interaction with delight but soon took on a more serious expression. "Say, Kirito…do you think this Noose of the Accursed might be possible to recast…or add new victims to somehow?"

"Uh…meaning, can she maintain the hundred who are already under the spell and cast the Noose on more players?"

"Yes," she said, totally serious. I was almost going to laugh it off, to say that it would practically be cheating to work like that.

But everyone's heads turned when a voice said, "Why not?"

Eleven pairs of eyes fixed on Argo's face. She continued, uncharacteristically severe, "In the Stiss Ruins, when Mutasina said their first target was Kirito's team, Dikkos of the Weed Eaters had said, 'Why would we do that? Use this choking magic on them and make them your slaves, too, why don't ya?'"

Indeed, that quote sounded like something I'd heard atop that stage in the ruins. But it was impressive that she could recall the details of the quote amid all the chaos of that scene.

"And Mutasina replied, 'It is not easy to succeed at casting the Noose of the Accursed. The motions are lengthy, and the magic circle is impossible to miss. It will not work this effectively without the right situation and audience, such as a group of people who would believe an easy lie about casting a grand buff spell on an entire gathering.' She didn't say that it was impossible for the spell to add extra targets to its effect. Of course, that coulda been a bluff to make her threat more effective…"

Another long silence settled over the scene. I was keenly aware of an itching around my throat where the symbol had been placed.

Asuna, who had brought up the topic, suggested, "It might be a bluff…but we should assume it's possible. Which means she might attempt to place the Noose upon us at some point, too. It might have lengthy motions and an obvious magic circle, but if the targets are surrounded with no escape…"

Her words brought the image of Mutasina to mind again.

She looked like a holy woman, wearing a spotless hooded white robe and bearing a simple staff, and her voice was pure and righteous, but the words she spoke were utterly cold and ruthless. She had called *SAO*, the world that Asuna and I and our friends lived through, *a world of pure hell that took four thousand lives with it, kicking and screaming.*

I had to take a deep breath to calm myself from the memory. "Yes, it's quite possible that Mutasina will attempt it...In fact, I can't imagine her doing anything else. She could clear out the forest around the town to prevent guerilla combat, surround us with a huge army to cut us off of escape, and then put the Noose on us. If that works, she'll earn herself sixty new followers."

"You know, I was thinking something," said Klein, still holding up his beer mug.

"Go ahead."

"You just said sixty—that includes the Bashin and the Patter, yeah? This might sound cold, but...will suffocation magic even work on NPCs who don't have physical players inside them?"

"Uh..." This question took me so by surprise that I had to blink several times before I could compose myself. "Um...While I know I said it was suffocating, it's not actually stopping the player's breath; it's just making it feel that way for the avatar, so..."

"Huh? Really?"

Now it was Klein's turn to be surprised. Even having experienced it for myself, I couldn't state for certain that it was safe. The recollection of that frighteningly realistic choking sensation came back to me, and I nearly started coughing out of sheer impulse.

"I conclude that it is impossible for an AmuSphere signal to stop actual physiological breathing," said Yui firmly.

She was being held in Lisbeth's lap at the moment and hopped up to walk over to me at the bulletin board, where she turned, white dress twirling, to continue her explanation.

"Respiratory control in the human body lies in the medulla oblongata, at the lower part of the brain stem. But the AmuSphere signals that allow a game program to interact with the brain only reach the cerebral cortex, the outermost layer of the brain. The cerebral cortex includes the sensory processing areas, so you might be able to create the illusion that breathing has stopped, but the AmuSphere is not functionally capable of stopping the body's respiration, and even if it were, the safety would kick in and forcefully log the player out of the system."

The collected group murmured with admiration at Yui's tactful, logical deduction. I had to take her word for it about the medulla oblongata and cerebral cortex, but I understood the final part of her speech very deeply. The AmuSphere was built directly in response to the NerveGear that took the lives of thousands of *SAO* players. It was packed with layers of safety features, so that if the user reached an unsafe heart rate, or went into a dehydrated state, or even just held their bladder for too long, they could be pulled out of the program. It was unthinkable that the people who made it would allow for any kind of freakish outcome that might have a direct effect on the user's life.

The Noose's feeling of constriction, like the sounds I was hearing and scents I was smelling, was nothing but a virtual sensory signal. But even still...

Yui continued, "Also, I surmise that the suffocation magic will be effective against NPCs like the Bashin and the Patter as well. NPCs in *Unital Ring* utilize the same language engine that I do. Through my avatar, I receive sensory information, including not just sight and hearing, but also smell, taste, and touch. I enjoy good smells and delicious flavors, but I am programmed to find pain and heat unpleasant in the same way that you all do. I was made indestructible in *SAO* and *ALO*, so I never felt pain in them, but now that I am a player, I will feel pain if I am slashed by a sword, and I will feel anguish if my windpipe is blocked."

Without thinking, I reached out toward Yui, rubbing her little head with my left hand. She smiled at my touch, reacting as though it was ticklish.

Yui could find delight in these interactions and think that

Asuna's cooking was delicious, but she could also feel physical pain and agony. The elaborate nature of Akihiko Kayaba's AI programming was as stunning as ever, yet I couldn't help but wonder why he hadn't just stopped at simulating the feeling of pleasure alone.

I didn't want to put Yui into our defensive battle, but I had a feeling she wouldn't accept that as an answer.

Klein smacked his knee to break the heavy silence. "Even if the suffocation spell works on NPCs and Yuippe, we can deal with it! If it's just an illusion, we can basically ignore it," he said confidently.

"Ah yes. If we know it's fake from the start, there's no need to panic about it," Leafa added. "In fact, our best chance to strike might be by allowing Mutasina to cast the magic on us. All the other enemies around us are going to fall over, so if we just withstand the pain and sprint to her, we could beat her with two or three good sword skills, right?"

That was my sister, ever the bold and confident combatant. In the Otherworld War, she had used the Terraria account to protect the Dark Territory's orcs and pugilists from thousands of American players, thanks to that spirit of hers.

However...

Unfortunately, the feeling of suffocation that the Noose of the Accursed simulated was horrifyingly difficult to bear, even knowing that it was just a virtual sensation. When I felt the effect of the Noose for myself in the coliseum of the Stiss Ruins, my first thought was what Yui had just said: *It had to be false, because the AmuSphere's safety systems made it impossible to stop the user's respiration.* But the feeling was so overwhelming that it shattered that logical thought process in an instant. The realistic sensation of having something stuck in my throat, impossible to swallow or spit out, caused a primal, biological panic. If she had waited five more seconds to turn off the spell's effect, I would have logged off to escape the terror of death.

Despite having experienced it already, and knowing that it was an illusion, I didn't think that I could ignore the effect and act with full and total movement. We ought to make our plans under the assumption that if the Noose was placed and activated, everyone under its effect would collapse to the ground on the spot.

But would the others believe me if I told them that now?

It was tempting to take on the Noose of the Accursed on purpose and launch an attack when Mutasina was expecting to have the advantage. It made it highly possible that we could keep our casualties to zero. And defeating Mutasina alone aligned with our core values better than an entire war. It made me wish that this was our only valid option—if only I hadn't experienced the suffocation for myself.

The group seemed likely to lean toward Klein's plan. I had to think of something to say that would convince them to go the other way...

I felt eyes on my cheek and turned to look directly into the gaze of Argo, who was seated cross-legged in the back row. The Rat's gold-tinged irises were telling me loud and clear, *Just give up and admit it already.*

...Oh, fine. Fine.

I exhaled and raised my hand.

"All right, folks, listen up. Unfortunately...I don't think that Klein's suggestion will work as well as you think."

"Why's that, Kiri, my man?" grumbled the katana-wielder.

I opened my ring menu, moved over to the equipment window, and removed the *Fine Iron Chest Armor*. Underneath, I wore only the *Ubiquicloth Undershirt* that Asuna had crafted, but it was a turtleneck style and nearly black in color, so it still wouldn't make the symbol of the Noose stand out, even if I pulled the collar down.

Throwing caution to the wind, I unequipped the undershirt, too, baring my torso. Leafa grimaced and exclaimed, "Hey, hang on, Big Brother! Why are you taking off...your...?"

She slowed down and trailed off as her wide eyes caught sight of what was on my throat. Everyone aside from Argo made the same expression.

"So yeah...This happened."

3

It was eleven PM, and we paused the meeting for a ten-minute bathroom break. Like my companions, I logged out.

I emerged from the game on my bed, staring up at the dark ceiling for several moments, waiting for the floating feeling to vanish.

I'd been prepared to suffer some major criticism for keeping secrets from the group when I revealed that I'd actually been hit by the Noose of the Accursed, but with Argo's assistance, I'd been spared their lectures for the time being. But as I feared, the topic of the session turned toward how to dispel the magic instead of the bigger picture, so I proposed that we take a quick break.

Time was too valuable to waste on getting rid of my sigil. If I was going to play until four in the morning, that left us with five hours to work with—and I wasn't positive we'd be able to finish the preparations for Mutasina's invasion.

"...If necessary, I might have to dive from school," I muttered, sitting up. I took off the AmuSphere and put the Augma on in its place, when a voice yelled "Big Brother!" and the door to my right burst open. It was Suguha, wearing a T-shirt and shorts. She'd bolted out of her room as soon as she logged out, judging by the AmuSphere in her hand.

"H-hey, you could at least—"

Knock, I was going to say, only to be interrupted by Suguha jumping onto my bed, pushing me back down. She straddled me on her knees, her chest thrust outward with indignation.

"*That's* the problem!"

"Wh-what is?" I asked.

Her eyebrows were sharp even at normal times, but now they were positively jagged with fury. "You know what! I mean your bad habit of taking on all the trouble by yourself! Like in the Underworld, with the max...maximum..."

"Maximum acceleration phase?"

"Yes, that! You were warned that if you didn't log out before that phase started, there would be consequences, but Asuna was there with you, and she said you never warned her about it!"

"B-because if I did, she would have insisted that she'd stay in the Underworld with me..."

"Even so, you *have to say it*!"

Suguha's eyes traveled slightly upward.

"You agree, don't you, Yui?!" she continued.

A tiny fairy flew down from above my head, putting her hands on her hips in midair just like Suguha, and made an adorable little version of an angry, scolding expression. "That's right, Papa! You should put more trust in Mama and Suguha and the rest of us!"

With my daughter in on the lecture, there was no longer any room for rebuttal.

"Y-you're right; I'm sorry. I thought it would worry you," I offered, putting my hands together in a sign of apology.

Yui moved up to sit on Suguha's shoulder. "Worrying about others and letting them worry about you is an important part of communication in a community, Papa."

"That's right, Big Brother. Obviously, it makes sense not to do things that will make others worry about you, but if something bad does happen, you have to be able to admit it and get help, rather than hiding it."

Suguha's lecture occupied my attention so fully that I only just now realized she had her Augma on, poking out below her bobbed hair. She must have telegraphed to Yui that they were going to raid my room before they logged out.

"You're right. I'm sorry. I've learned my lesson. I'll talk to people about these things next time," I announced again.

My sister glowered down at me. "Swear to Stacia?"

"S-swear to Stacia."

"Good!"

At last, her face crinkled into a smile, and Suguha got off of me, sitting down on an empty spot on the bed. She didn't seem intent on leaving, so I went ahead and asked, without any tact, "Don't you need to use the toilet?"

"I already did. Maybe *you* should go."

"Y-yeah, I will…"

I got my feet on the floor, and Suguha added, "Bring back some sparkling water from the fridge, too! The lime flavor!"

"Yeah, yeah," I groaned, exiting to the hallway. I started heading for the bathroom but noticed Yui flying just on my left. "Um, Miss Yui…I'm about to use the restroom…," I whispered, which took the pixie by surprise at first.

"Oh! I'm sorry, Papa!" she stammered. "I just had something for your ears only…"

"What is it?"

"Take a look at this," she said, showing me a holo-window. It was a real-time display of my vital signs, with numbers and graphs for temperature, blood pressure, and heart rate. The microsensor implanted in my chest was sending the information to the Augma.

This sensor was implanted—at a specialty hospital, of course—when I was about to perform the job of STL test diver for the Oceanic Resource Exploration and Research Institution, better known as Rath, at their recommendation. Now that the job was technically over, I could have it removed, but I'd chosen not to, for three reasons. One, because it would hurt. Two, I didn't have to put on a heart monitor when riding a bike for exercise. And three, because Asuna liked being able to monitor my vital signs, for some reason.

I felt oddly embarrassed about having my temperature and heart rate visible, but I found it difficult to say, "No more." So I left the sensor where it was. But why was that data coming into play now...?

Yui gave me the rapid-fire answer to that question. "This is your vital data starting from 10:18:35 last night, Papa."

"After ten...?" I repeated, wondering what I was doing at that point.

Then I recalled that it was when Argo and I were sneaking into the meetup of *ALO* players at the coliseum in the center of the Stiss Ruins. I was fighting off the temptation of the buffet feast and thinking of slipping away when Mutasina cast a massive spell from the stage. Yes, 10:18 was the very minute that the Noose stopped my breathing.

Stunned, I looked at where Yui was pointing out the bottom of the three line graphs: my heart rate.

"Unfortunately, the sensor chip implanted in your chest cannot monitor the number of breaths you've taken, so there's no way to determine whether the Noose of the Accursed actually stopped your respiration. But you can see that your heart rate shot upward here."

"Yes, I see...But that's normal, isn't it? Your heart rate goes up a fair amount even when fighting monsters, so while the sensation is virtual, it's natural that feeling like you can't breathe will cause your heart to hammer away..."

"That's not the problem," she said seriously, shaking her head. "The AmuSphere's safety restriction system is designed to activate if the user's heart rate passes a certain maximum threshold for at least five seconds. The threshold is set to be two hundred and twenty, minus the user's age. So, in your case, it would be two hundred and three."

"Two hundred and two, next week," I noted pointlessly.

"Indeed," Yui replied, obliging me for a split second. "But look here. Your pulse rose to two hundred and five at 10:18:41, then dropped to a hundred and ninety-five after four seconds. At 0:48

seconds, it rose to two hundred and four, then dropped after four seconds again, to the hundred and nineties. At 0:55 seconds, it descended back to a normal pulse."

"...Uh-huh..."

The pulse graph showed exactly what Yui pointed out. I'd passed the maximum threshold twice, but both cases lasted just under the five seconds needed to detach me from the system. I was alarmed by the numbers themselves, but the safety mechanisms were working normally, it seemed.

"So what's the problem?"

"Your heart rate crossed the safety threshold twice within twenty seconds, but both times, it decreased after four seconds. I feel that the specificity of the four-second period is artificial in nature."

"Artificial...You mean, because both times it dropped just before it reached the five-second cutoff? But that could just be a coincidence, right? This heart rate graph is based on my chest sensor's readings, not the AmuSphere's, and there shouldn't be any way for the AmuSphere itself to control my heart rate."

"That is accurate. However," Yui cautioned, "even if it was sheer coincidence that your heart rate dropped twice after four seconds, if the same magic is cast on a hundred people in the same place, more than a few of them ought to have tripped the safety threshold and been forcibly logged out by their devices. When the Noose of the Accursed was activated, did you notice any players disconnecting around you?"

"......Um..."

I gazed into the gloom at the end of the hallway, using it as a screen to envision what I had seen. While the Noose was active, I had been so desperate to eject the object stuck in my throat that I didn't have the wherewithal to look around me, but despite that, I couldn't recall any light or sound that accompanied the logging-out effect. After the suffocating sensation vanished, the density of the crowd in the coliseum was the same as before the spell was activated.

"...No. I can't be certain...But I don't think that anyone was removed from the game from an emergency shutdown..."

"I see...," Yui replied, but that was it. She closed the holo-window and rose higher. "I'm sorry to have interrupted your bathroom trip, Papa. Take your time."

I felt a little bit self-conscious hearing that from Yui, who had no need for the restroom, but there was no time to waste—only four minutes left in the break.

"A-all right. Go on back to the room."

"I will!"

She flew off with a twinkling sound, passing right through the door, at which point I turned and sprinted for the bathroom.

I washed my hands and face at the sink, then went to the kitchen to grab the lime-flavored sparkling water for Suguha and a bottle of oolong tea for myself before returning to my room. The entire while, I thought about what Yui had shown me.

If the heart rate of all one hundred people at the scene had dropped just before the safety measures kicked in, then Mutasina's suffocation magic somehow knew the maximum allowable pulse in each player's AmuSphere—and could limit their heartbeats so they did not cross that value for five full seconds.

I could hardly believe such a thing was possible. Since the maximum rate was 220 minus the player's age, the number would be different for each player, and even if you could acquire that number, it wasn't the brain that controlled the heart's palpitation rate, but an area of the heart itself called the sinoatrial node. There was no way the AmuSphere's microwaves could reach that far.

There must have been something I was missing. If Mutasina's spell was controlling something, it wouldn't be the heartbeat itself...but something related to it, such as...

"You took too long, Big Brother!" shouted the voice that made me realize I'd gotten back to my room. Suguha was sitting there on the bed, waving her hands to beckon me over. "Only ninety seconds left!"

"Sorry, sorry. But they aren't going to flip out over a minute or two of delay..."

"That's no example for the leader to set!"

"F-for one thing, I'm not officially the leader...," I argued weakly, handing her the bottle of water. The sparkling water that we always had a healthy stock of at the house required some hard wrist work to open, but my kendo-practicing sister had no trouble breaking the seal and furiously downing the water. She made a childish grimace as the carbonation tore at her throat and then ejected the carbon dioxide as daintily as one could before putting the cap back on and setting the bottle on the headboard.

"One more minute! Hurry, hurry, hurry!"

Suguha went to lie down on the bed, and I hastily pulled the oolong tea away from my lips.

"Really? Are you going to dive in here again?"

"It's your fault for coming back so late. Plus, just in case, if Mutasina's magic really does make you stop breathing, I have to perform lifesaving measures on you."

I wasn't sure how serious she was being, but I couldn't just laugh off a statement like that. Yui, floating nearby, nodded seriously.

"If that happens, you have to take care of Papa, Leafa!"

"I got ya covered!"

Seeing them back each other up made me realize just how long the two of them had known each other.

Back in the log cabin, there were thirty seconds left in our break period, but everyone was already online again. It was after eleven o'clock, but there was a bristling enthusiasm coming from the entire group that said we were just getting started.

It made sense that they were motivated. Before Mutasina made her nature known to the genial gathering of *ALO* players (and Argo and me), the mood was very friendly. I didn't sense any hostility from the hundred motivated players there. Meaning that if we beat Mutasina in a direct fight, there shouldn't be anyone left who'd want to attack Ruis na Ríg. With that hurdle cleared, we'd be free to challenge *Unital Ring* without any extra anxiety.

Thinking back on it, however, Mocri's party that tried to kill me that first night had mentioned something about a mysterious "Sensei" who might have been egging them on, and it was possible that the same was true for Schulz's team, Fawkes, that attacked the cabin the second night.

When my three-part sword skill hit Schulz, he had uttered a few enigmatic words before he was permanently banished from the realm.

Kirito...you're...really...

His avatar disappeared right at that moment, so I couldn't hear the rest of what he was going to say. I had a feeling it was going to end in a question, perhaps in surprise that I hadn't been what he expected. If that information was false, something fed to him—and the person who said it was the same Sensei who'd taught Mocri and his friends PvP combat...then someone was manipulating the former *ALO* players in an attempt to get them to wipe us out of *Unital Ring*.

Would that person happen to be the leader of the Virtual Study Society, Mutasina? Or was that witch also under this Sensei's control...?

I stood on the spot where I'd logged in, pondering this, when someone smacked me hard on the back.

"Yo, Kiri, my man, everyone's here! What's up? Should we continue what we were discussing before?"

"Huh? Oh, right...," I stammered, looking up at Klein, who was wearing his trademark bandana. But I came to my senses and shook my head. "Um, no, let's not."

I turned to the others, all standing in the center of the living room, and announced, "May I have a moment? As far as our plans go...I honestly think that searching for a way to undo the power of the Noose of the Accursed on our own would be a waste of time."

Several protests arose at once. I appreciated their concern for my sake, but we had a higher priority at the moment.

"I'm not saying I don't think there's a way. There was dispelling magic and potions and items in *ALO*, so it wouldn't be a surprise at all if such things exist here as well. But we're totally lacking in knowledge about magic skills right now, and even if we discovered the way, a massive spell that can choke a hundred people at once is naturally going to require an equally high-level method to undo. There's no way we can get the proficiency high enough to pull that off in just a day—no, half a day."

This time, there were no arguments.

But I could see the strained looks on their faces, as though they were all suffering the Noose for themselves. They probably *were* feeling that way, in all honesty. They were the best companions I could ever ask for, and that was why I didn't want to lose a single one on the way to finishing this game. To do so would require the greatest possible effort—without harming my school studies, of course—before Mutasina's army attacked.

I nodded slowly to the group and got to the most crucial point.

"Just as hard as dispelling the Noose of the Accursed would be to ignore its effects. It's difficult to describe in words…But when she activates the spell, it truly feels like you're suffocating, like there's a big sticky lump stuck in your throat. You can't exhale or inhale, and of course, you can't talk, either. If you suck in a huge breath and hold it right before the spell is activated, you might be able to last on that for part of a minute…But all she needs to do is strike the ground with her staff, so you'd have to keep a close eye on her movements at all times, and that's not possible in a battle. Unfortunately, I think that Klein and Leafa's suggestion that we succumb to the Noose in order to get up close and strike isn't going to work out."

Slowly, I exhaled the breath from my avatar's virtual lungs.

If you thought about it, air didn't actually exist in any virtual world. The scent of wood in the log cabin, the chill of the night breeze coming through the open window—these were sensations the AmuSphere was sending directly to our brains. There wasn't a single molecule of gas carrying any smell or temperature in the environment. The same was true for the sensation of air passing through our mouths, throats, and lungs when we breathed. In a sense, this world was a more perfect vacuum than even the actual vacuum of outer space. But knowing that this was true was not going to help anyone overcome that horrifyingly real sense of suffocation. The inability to breathe was one of those experiences that was simply encoded into the human soul as a primal fear…

"But, Kirito, how do you intend for us to fight against an army of a hundred?" said a soft voice, drawing my attention back to the room and the people in it.

It was Alice, who stood directly across from me. The knight's blue eyes stared right into mine without blinking.

If I was going to rule out Klein and Leafa's plan to intentionally suffer the Noose, I had to offer an alternative idea. A plan that would bring us victory without losing any of our own, the Bashin, the Patter, the pets, or more than a minimum of enemy deaths.

"…I want to avoid a head-on confrontation with a hundred-strong army," I replied.

"I know," said Klein, "but Yui already predicted that Mutasina's army is gonna cut down all the trees around Ruis na Ríg. If you have two huge raid parties meeting in a flat, open area, it's gonna come down to direct combat, ya know?"

"Yes, I assume so. Which means…"

Over a span of fifteen minutes, I explained the idea that I'd been turning over in my mind from the moment I learned that Mutasina and her army of a hundred would be attacking our town.

There were many questions, but I ultimately won everyone's approval, and we decided to begin preparing for the plan at eleven thirty. Before that, however, we got together for some tea and snacks for a little morale boost.

The beer that had been served at the feast hours earlier was pro-vided in great amount by the *Insectsite* gang, but there was none left (due to Klein's bottomless stomach) and I didn't know where they got the stuff. I liked it, too—I was still a minor, but it wasn't illegal for me to drink in a virtual world—so I hoped to learn how they got it and acquire some for myself once we had defeated Mutasina's army. For now, I sipped our oddly flavored tea.

After this, Argo and I would act separately from the group. My SP and TP were topped off, so I headed for the door to set off before the others but was interrupted by Lisbeth clapping her hands.

"All right, everyone! Attention, please!"

What was this? Lisbeth was standing in front of the board, with Silica and Leafa on her right; Sinon, Alice, and Argo on her left; and Yui pushing Asuna into the center of the living room. Asuna seemed just as mystified by this as I was.

Next, all the aforementioned girls opened their menus and went to the inventory. Then they paused, timed themselves ("Ready, set—"), and shouted...

"Happy birthday, Asuna!!"

The group materialized *something*, all at once.

It was a massive proliferation of tiny colorful objects: flowers. An eruption of flowers piled atop their windows, which the seven of them scooped up with both hands and tossed at Asuna. The many-colored petals fell around her like snowflakes, filling the living room with their sweet scent.

Klein, Agil, and Hyme weren't aware this surprise was coming, either, but they rallied at once and broke into applause. Asuna looked upward, blinking with surprise, at the rain of petals around her, then put on a dazzling smile.

"Liz, Silica, Leafa, Shino-non, Yui, Argo, and Alice...thank you all so much."

I joined in the applause, determined not to be left behind, and couldn't help but think, *I'm so glad that Mutasina's invasion wasn't tonight...*

4

Argo and I left Ruis na Ríg with Kuro at our side, and we made our way carefully through the deep forest around us.

We already knew there were no truly dangerous monsters in this area, but there were still nocturnal animal-type monsters like foxes and bats that bothered us along the way. We weren't trying to level up, so I intended to avoid them whenever possible and only fight when needed—but to my surprise, a single growl from Kuro sent nearly every one of them fleeing. Apparently, the panther had some kind of intimidation skill.

The original plan was to dedicate half our time tonight to leveling up and skill proficiency, but fortunately for us, that was no longer necessary. Defeating the mega-difficult field boss, the Life Harvester, gave each of us a minimum of two levels.

That put our present level, class, and ability tree status as follows.

KIRITO
Level-20, 1H Swords / Decay Magic / Blacksmith / Carpentry / Stoneworking / Woodworking / Tamer (Brawn)

SINON
Level-18, Gunner / Thief / Stoneworking / Woodworking / Herbalist (Swiftness)

ALICE
Level-18, Bastard Swords / Pottery / Weaving / Tailoring (Brawn)

LEAFA
Level-16, Bastard Swords / Woodworking / Pottery (Brawn)

LISBETH
Level-15, Maces / Blacksmith / Carpentry / Weaving / Pottery
(Toughness)

SILICA
Level-15, Short Swords / Tamer / Weaving / Scouting
(Swiftness)

YUI
Level-14, Daggers / Fire Magic / Cooking / Weaving (Sagacity)

ASUNA
Level-14, Rapiers / Herbalist / Cooking / Woodworking / Pottery /
Weaving / Tailoring / Tamer (Sagacity)

ARGO
Level-14, Short Swords / Scouting / Thief / Herbalist (Swiftness)

KLEIN
Level-13, Curved Blades / Woodworking / Stoneworking (Brawn)

AGIL
Level-13, Axes / Woodworking / Stoneworking (Toughness)

HYME
Level-16, Scythes / Stoneworking / Woodworking / Herbalist
(Swiftness)

MISHA
Thornspike cave bear, Level-8

KURO
Lapispine dark panther, Level-7

AGA
Long-billed giant agamid, Level-6

PINA
Feathery dragon, Level-7

The reason the group had so many professions was because simply earning the corresponding skill would make it show up on your status screen. You could earn the Stoneworking skill just by picking up two rocks and smacking them together. I doubted that qualified one to be called a stoneworker, but Argo was guessing that as you racked up skill proficiency, you'd eventually be forced to sort and choose from your skills.

What I found interesting was that Hyme the praying mantis was given the class of scythe-user. According to her, in *Insectsite*, players' main weapons were their natural assets, so if you were a stag beetle, you'd use your jaw to perform Great Pincers sword skills, while a rhinoceros beetle's horn would do Cudgel sword skills, and a praying mantis's arms would do Scythe sword skills.

Of course, prior to the game conversion, there were no sword skills in *Insectsite*, so they were still at less than a 50 percent success rate when attempting to execute a skill on the first try. That rate would increase with practice, I assumed, but it was clear that being from *ALO* gave us the blessing of experience when it came to familiarity with sword skills.

But in fact, the presence of sword skills in *ALO* was an irregular occurrence already, due to the end of RCT Progress, the original publisher of the game. In truth, the ones who had the biggest advantage in *Unital Ring* weren't the *ALO* players...

I shook my head, dispelling that line of thought. It was time to focus on the task at hand.

We snuck carefully and quietly through the dark of night. Mutasina's attack was supposed to be tomorrow night, but there was no guarantee that they didn't have an advance party in place already.

"Hey, Kiri-boy, what about there?" whispered a voice off to the right. I came to a stop, as did Kuro, who was silently stalking on my left, and sniffed the night air.

"Which way is 'there'?" I asked, taking a step closer to Argo. A pale hand pointed through the darkness beyond the trees. The storm had passed hours earlier, but the sky was still mostly clouded over; if I didn't have the Night Vision skill, I wouldn't be able to see more than ten feet ahead.

Squinting through the gloom, I could make out the rushing Maruba River past the trees and the spacious riverbed. We'd picked our way through the trees rather than the easy path of the riverbed to cut down on the chances of encountering any scout parties. If other players were approaching, Kuro would probably sniff them out before Argo or I saw them, but caution was imperative. If the enemy just so happened to spot us, we'd have to rebuild our strategy from scratch.

The three of us were hiding out at a spot close to two miles south of Ruis na Ríg. Another mile, and we'd reach the southern tip of the Great Zelletelio Forest, but leaving was beside the point. We needed to find the right spot inside the woods.

"Hmm, it's too far to make out well," I grumbled, straining my eyes.

Argo chuckled. "You oughtta grind out more Night Vision proficiency. The best way to raise it I've found is tryin' to read in darkness."

"That seems like it would lower your vision instead," I grumbled, just as a wide, short window popped open in front of my face: *Night Vision skill proficiency has risen to 6.*

The clarity of my sight rose just a small bit, bringing the landscape through the trees into better relief.

The Maruba River was a majestic one, over a hundred yards across if you included the whole riverbed. My home city of Kawagoe meant "crossing the rivers," one of which was the Iruma River. Where it ran closest to my house, the riverbed was two hundred yards across, but looking at this one, it felt like it was about the same size.

The spot Argo was pointing out, however, was less than half as wide as elsewhere along the river, because the forest table was pressing inward from both sides. I thought I recalled that we passed this narrow spot going down to the Stiss Ruins with Alice last night, and I had reminded myself to pay close attention, lest we take a tumble into the water due to reduced mobility.

"...Seems good," I murmured.

Proudly, Argo replied, "Don't it?" Not that *she* created that spot, I thought, but she was the one who found it first, so I gave her a begrudging "GJ" and continued forward.

Just before we emerged from the forest, we checked to make sure no other players were nearby. After our eyes and Kuro's nose and ears turned up nothing, I declared it safe and opened my ring menu.

As in the old *SAO*, the system window drew a fair bit of attention in the dark. Although no monsters swarmed over to the light of the window, it would stand out to players. So you could use it as a signal to your friends, but it might also give away your location to criminal orange players—so it was common knowledge among solo players that you had to carefully ensure your window's illumination didn't travel a long distance.

There should be no players around to notice this light, but even still, I placed the menu behind a tree trunk and quickly opened my map. By holding a long press on my current location, I placed a red X mark on the map there.

With this task complete, I promptly closed my menu and exhaled with relief. A cloth pouch hanging from my belt held some bison jerky, which I gave to Kuro as a treat. "The real problem is time," I murmured. "If we start too early, it'll break down before we put the plan into motion, and if it's too late, it won't be ready in time..."

"That's true...," murmured Argo. "I'm thinkin' we need to be starting on our idea right around the time Mutasina's army leaves the Stiss Ruins. It's a hundred people crossin' eighteen miles, so it'll take three hours, even if they run the whole way. In fact, if you run in *UR*, you're losin' TP and SP fast. So considering fuel, it'd be more like a four-hour jog…"

"And if it takes us an hour to set up our trap, that leaves a three-hour gap. I *think* it should hold up fine for that long…But there's no saying with these things until you make it."

"And considering the amount of resources it'll take, there's no way to test it out first."

"Yeah…"

Right now, our friends were working hard around Ruis na Ríg, packing their item storage full of resources. The plan that I envisioned called for a vast amount of materials, so there was no way for us to build one first just to test its durability. I was certain the mechanism itself would work—the question was how many hours it would hold.

If this were the Underworld, I could use Incarnation power to create something that would last ten *years* without budging, I thought ruefully. The idea put a figure into my mind, someone framed against the evening sun coming through the car window, with a cylindrical uniform cap and wavy flaxen hair…

It took considerable force of will to hold back the sudden flood of emotion. I needed to focus on *this* world. Thinking too much about the Underworld while in *Unital Ring* was going to make me accidentally try to block a sword attack with Incarnation, with disastrous results.

"…Now that I'm thinking about it, Argo, we don't know for sure when Mutasina's group is leaving the Stiss Ruins, do we?" I pointed out.

The info agent snorted. "Don't insult me, boy. I've already identified about twenty individual social media accounts belonging to members of the Weed Eaters, Absolute Survivor Squad, and Announcer Fan Club, all of whom were assimilated into Mutasina's army. I'll know when they're on the move, because all their accounts'll go silent at the same time."

"……Wow…Good thinking…"

I couldn't hate on that logic. I'd been both bailed out and

made a fool of by her incredible information network in the *SAO* days—so it was good to have her on my side now.

"…By the way, Argo," I asked incidentally. "I couldn't help noticing you're pretty good with English. Where did you learn it…?"

The Rat reached under her hood and rubbed between her nose and lip. "Hmmm, that'll cost ya about two hundred el."

"Two hundred…That's so expensive! A whole shish kebab costs just three dim! And a hundred dim is one el, so I could buy six thousand six hundred and sixty-six kebabs for the cost of that secret!" I shouted, then clamped my hands over my mouth. I would look like the biggest idiot in the world if I got spotted by their scouts for this.

Fortunately, the only response was a cry of *hruffoo* from a mystery bird in the branches overhead. Much quieter, I added, "If I ever get my hands on some one hundred-el silver coins, I'm gonna buy that intel off of you."

"Heh-heh, I look forward to it. It'll be a while yet, though. Monsters in this world don't drop coins as a general rule."

"…That's true."

As Argo said, the animals we'd been fighting like bears, bison, frogs, and bats dropped plenty of material items, but not a single coin. The NPC shop inside the Stiss Ruins *did* buy all of my extra, unwanted materials for money, but the total price was three el, seventy-eight dim. If I was acquiring about an el per day, I'd need two hundred days to save up enough.

"And the Life Harvester didn't drop any money, either…," I grumbled.

"But it dropped tons and tons o' stuff," Argo shot back. "I bet you'd make a pretty good pile o' cash from selling all of it."

"I guess…"

As a matter of fact, in addition to so much raw meat we couldn't possibly use all at once, the Life Harvester also dropped a huge amount of material items. Not just its carapace and bones, but teeth, tendons, secretions, calculi, eyeballs, and other such errata. We placed them in the log cabin's storage, but we hadn't yet decided what to do with them. Like Argo said, we could carry them to the Stiss Ruins and sell them off, but my gamer's instincts raged against the idea of simply selling boss materials to a shop.

"...In other games, you'd eventually need that stuff to make some kind of epic weapon...But I don't know if that logic holds true here as well..."

"I mean, it's all bones and eyeballs and stuff. No idea what skill even makes use of 'em, so my guess is that they'll do ya better if converted to cash than rotting away in your inventory."

"I'm guessing there's some NPC somewhere who can make gear out of biological materials," I commented. But a thought struck my brain. "Wait...Why don't we just ask an NPC, then? The Bashin are using pelt armor and bone weapons, right? They must know how to refine the materials."

"...Good point. Well, shucks, shoulda done some intel gathering during the feast...Can't believe I missed that opportunity..."

"Well, neither of us can speak Bashin."

"I already got a proficiency of five in the Bashin language—and three in Patter."

"......Congrats," I said, making a little pose of resignation before I got to my feet. "Well, let's head back and join in the harvesting. We don't know how much we'll need in the end, after all..."

"True."

With one last shared bob of the head, the Rat, the panther, and I hurried back the way we'd come, on the animal trail through the woods.

5

Thursday, October 1st.

The autumn sun shone down from a clear blue sky, brightening the left half of the classroom. The open windows ushered in a slight breeze carrying the sounds of the city outside, which in turn mixed with the sound of the students' ceaseless styluses.

Long ago, before I knew who I really was, I felt excited about the arrival of October. I was allowed to request the two big presents I got each year, so I started thinking in August about what to get for my October 7th birthday. Sometimes I got my very first choice, and sometimes they nixed all the way through my third backup option, but regardless, I always counted down the days with anticipation.

But the year that I learned I wasn't actually born as a member of the Kirigaya family, I stopped asking for presents. When Mom would ask what I wanted, I'd brush her off by saying, "Anything's fine." When she went to the trouble of picking out new sneakers or a backpack, I'd stick the gifts in my closet and refuse to use them. That attitude lasted until my second year of middle school, when I was trapped in *SAO* a month after my fourteenth birthday.

In November, two years later, I was freed from the death game. The day before my birthday last year, Mom and Suguha asked me what I wanted for my birthday. Even now, I could feel the stabbing pang of remorse that overtook me at that moment. At the time, I very nearly apologized for my childish attitude but realized it wasn't something that should be done out of sheer momentum. So I considered their question carefully and replied, "Anything's fine." I believed that although my words were the same, they understood that the emotion behind those words couldn't have been more different. Whatever the present was, I would treasure it for life. Not by preserving it on a shelf, but by actually using it…just as I used the bike they gave me to celebrate starting the semester at the returnee school in April.

"Next…Kirigaya, why don't you read?"

"Y-yes, ma'am!" I said automatically, my attention pulled back to the class. I got to my feet.

Mrs. Yorita, the teacher of our required world history class, had explained during her introduction that she was born the year that President Kennedy was assassinated. Her tall and slender form did not look like it was sixty-three years old, however. Her lower, husky voice and masculine manner made her popular with the girls, but her primary skill was detecting mental distraction in her students, because she had a very strong track record of calling on people who weren't fully concentrating on the lesson.

Sadly, my desk neighbors were not nice girls who would whisper the section to read under their breath for me, but guys who thought it was funny when you got called on by the teacher. I'd seen a number of my classmates get witheringly embarrassed in front of the class for this sort of thing already, so I made sure to keep half of my mind focused on the lesson at all times. I cleared my throat and began to read from the digital textbook on my tablet.

"…Meanwhile, in America, President Franklin Roosevelt, elected in 1932, pushed for his New Deal movement, which would strengthen governmental control over the banking industry…"

—◆—

After the morning classes, Asuna quickly put away her tablet and left the classroom in a hurry, carrying the large insulated bag under her arm.

The bag was keeping five homemade sandwiches cool. She didn't have enough time to make anything fancier than ham, cheese, and tomato; egg and broccoli; and olive and tuna, but she knew her friends would love them.

She offered to bring lunch for the group partially to repay everyone for their birthday surprise last night and partially so they could make good use of their valuable lunch break. Buying lunch at the crowded cafeteria would take at least ten minutes. But this way, they could spend a full forty minutes out of the fifty-minute lunch period on their strategy meeting.

The five-minute travel time to and from the meeting was because it was being held not in the cafeteria or the "secret garden," but in the computing lab on the third floor of Building Two. It wasn't the ideal location for a lunch, but secrecy was of the utmost importance today. There was still a greater-than-zero chance that one of those hundred *ALO* players compelled to join Mutasina's army was a student at our school, and the last thing we wanted was for them to find out the details of the plan to fight them off.

To get to Building Two, Asuna had to go down from the third floor of Building One to the second floor, then cross the elevated walkway. She made haste along the way, looking for Lisbeth (Rika Shinozaki) and Argo (Tomo Hosaka) along the same route, but they must have gotten ahead of her while she was putting her tablet away and getting the insulated bag from her locker.

They're both so impatient. She chuckled to herself, right as she was about to descend the stairs.

"Miss Yuuki," said a voice, causing Asuna to stop.

She turned around, feeling slightly nervous, to see a girl wearing a uniform that did not belong to this school.

She wore a gray blazer with navy blue lapels. A pleated skirt so crisp that the folds were like knife blades. Shiny black hair, reserved features…It was the transfer student who had come to the returnee school just four days ago: Shikimi Kamura.

"Hello, Miss Kamura," Asuna replied with a smile and a bow. Shikimi grinned and returned the greeting.

"Are you having lunch now? If it's not a bother, would you mind if I joined you?"

"Um, well…"

Asuna had to think quickly about how to respond.

She couldn't be absent from the lunch meeting. It was a crucial opportunity to sit face-to-face and discuss their plan, and if she didn't bring her sandwiches, Kazuto and the others would go without any lunch.

On the other hand, she couldn't invite Shikimi to the computing lab. The girl wouldn't be a *Unital Ring* player—or any VRMMO, surely—so it would be very poor form to bring her along and then ignore her to talk about strategy. She'd have to decline for today.

Asuna sucked in the breath she would use to apologize and say she already had plans, but the air caught in her throat.

She'd noticed a pin on Shikimi's uniform lapel, a stylized combination of the letter *A* and a rose. It was the insignia of Eterna Girls' Academy, the private school Asuna had previously attended.

Shikimi claimed that she had transferred from Eterna to the returnee school because it would give her a topic for the English essay she'd need to attend college in America. The essay required a strong personal angle, so the choice to experience the returnee school, which was perhaps unique among all schools in the entire world, made a kind of sense. But the content of Shikimi's essay would probably end up being about how she came into contact with a student who'd suffered mental trauma from the *SAO* Incident and how she helped them cope—or something like that. She might even write about this experience today. "I thought we were friends, but she refused to eat lunch with me. You can see how tall the defensive walls these *SAO* survivors build around their hearts are…"

It was a stupid thing to think, and she knew it. But she couldn't stop the thoughts that came flooding out of her.

The *Unital Ring* incident was a truly astounding shake-up, but it was still just a game. Asuna was using a game as the reason to refuse to spend time with a transfer student who still had few friends at this school. When she was in Eterna Girls' Academy's middle school, before the *SAO* Incident, would she have made the same choice? No, she would have prioritized spending time with a new friend in real life over something in a game, no matter how impactful it was…

The actual amount of time that Asuna spent unable to respond couldn't have been more than half a second. But it was enough for Shikimi to shrug, seeing directly through Asuna's mind at her thoughts.

"I'm sorry to have bothered you. It was coming out of nowhere, wasn't it?"

"Uh…no…"

"Don't let it bother you. What about lunch tomorrow, instead?"

"…Yes, I'd love to," Asuna replied. Shikimi beamed, then bowed again and stepped nimbly down the stairs.

Asuna waited until she had gone down to the landing and back around before starting downward herself. Everyone was surely at the computing lab already by now, but her legs felt heavy.

Why did talking with this girl make her feel so confused and conflicted? Shikimi was nothing less than gentle and polite, and nothing she did seemed malicious in any way. It had to be a problem with Asuna. There was something in Shikimi's profile, as a student hoping to go from Eterna Girls' Academy's high school to a university overseas, that made her think, *That could have been me.*

Asuna had no regrets over the impulsive decision to put on her brother's NerveGear helmet in the fall of her third year of middle school. She'd experienced the fear of death many times in Aincrad and gone through many hard and painful things, but there had been just as many fun and happy memories. If she hadn't been trapped in *SAO*, she'd never have met Lisbeth, Argo, Yui, and Kirito.

She didn't feel the tiniest bit of dissatisfaction over who she was now. Whatever the future held in store for her, she knew she could make her way directly through what lay ahead, as long as she had her connections to her friends, Yui, and Kirito.

And yet…why?

But this wasn't the time to be asking that question. It might only be a game to Shikimi, but to Asuna, the Seed Nexus was another reality entirely. She had no choice but to win the battle tonight to ensure that they protected the log cabin that had played host to so many memories and got it back home to Alfheim at some point.

Once she reached the second floor of the school building, Asuna made her way through the foot traffic of students walking toward the cafeteria and rushed down the connecting hallway.

—◊◊◊—

Welcome back; you're late, Big Brother!

I opened the glass door to our house, expecting to hear Suguha's voice as soon as I got inside.

But my sister wasn't at the door. Her shoes weren't in the lowered entryway, either, so I had gotten home first today, it seemed.

That was normal, though. Her commute time was only half of mine, but Suguha was a regular on the kendo team, so naturally she had practice after school. She'd been taking rest days and leaving early recently to ensure she got home before five o'clock, but as the vice captain of the team, she couldn't skip out on the others like that all the time.

Fortunately, she seemed to be getting along with the rest of the team, as far as I could tell. But on the other hand, I'd never seen Suguha in her official capacity as a kendo team member; I felt my resolve to cheer her on at the newcomer competition next month renewed. I used the restroom, washed my hands and face at the sink, and headed to the kitchen. I'd bought three fruit puddings at a dessert shop on the way home, so I stuck two in the refrigerator and took the third to the table to eat. Ordinarily, I almost never bought snacks to eat for myself, but I needed all the energy I could get before our big battle in a few hours.

Argo hadn't sent a warning from monitoring the social media accounts of Mutasina's army members, so they hadn't left the Stiss Ruins yet. Since there were students and workers in that group, they'd probably be leaving around eight o'clock, and if we counted three hours or so for travel, the fight should happen around eleven. I had to wonder what they would do if they attacked at that point and we weren't there…But Mutasina would probably prefer to destroy an empty Ruis na Ríg, for all I knew.

That was a big question: Why did that witch want to crush us anyway? Was it simply because we were the *ALO* players who were the closest to the "land revealed by the heavenly light"? Or did she have another reason? I wanted to ask her myself, but because our victory was sealed by killing her, the only chance I would have to ask was if we lost the battle, but I survived. As a frontline damage dealer, losing usually meant being the first to die—so in any case, I doubted I'd have the chance to talk.

Once again, I heard Mutasina's words at the Stiss Ruins ringing in my ears.

The darkness SAO *gave birth to has only spread throughout the Seed Nexus and multiplied. Now those infinite worlds have coalesced into one. In* Unital Ring, *the darkness will be compressed again, and when its density surpasses its peak, something new will result…something even darker and deeper. And I want to see that.*

I found it hard to take her words seriously, but it was true that there had been both light and darkness in *SAO*. If the links between Asuna, Lisbeth, Silica, Klein, Agil, Argo, me, and so many others were the light, then things like the PK guild Laughing Coffin were the malicious darkness.

And because Laughing Coffin had become a kind of legend,

its followers—its cultish believers—could be found in all kinds of VRMMOs. The Seed Package allowed for PKing as a general rule, but killing another person was much harder to do, mentally speaking, in a full-dive environment. So if some today found it fascinating that a few people were killing players left and right in *SAO*, where death was permanent, then that might indeed represent the "darkness *SAO* gave birth to," in my opinion.

When Mutasina prophesied that the darkness would be compressed in *Unital Ring*, what did that mean? That the multitudes of Seed VRMMO players arranged at the rim of this vast continent would fight each other harder and harder as they grew closer to the center of the world.

First players from the same world would fight one another, then they would grapple with players from adjacent worlds, with everyone killing each other until the winner reached the land revealed by the heavenly light: the final group…or perhaps final individual.

It reminded me of the legendary Chinese poison supposedly created by pitting various poisonous creatures against each other, until only the last survived with the most potent form of all. Hundreds of thousands of players converted over from other games, all dead, with only one winner standing tall in the end. Was that what Mutasina wanted? To absorb into herself that "something even darker and deeper," and become "something new"…?

"…It's just a game," I muttered to myself, lifting the final spoonful to my mouth. The pudding cost a whole 350 yen per serving, and it was rich enough to be worth it; I focused on the flavor to reset my thoughts. Whoever set up the *Unital Ring* incident, the winner wasn't suddenly going to develop superhuman powers. The statement in the announcement about "all shall be given" was probably just referring to in-game items or stats or, at most, some real money.

My reason for seeking out the land revealed by the heavenly light was different from Mutasina's. I wanted to know who had done this thing, and I wanted to send the data for my character and my friends' back to *ALO*, along with our log cabin. While combat with other players might be unavoidable, I had no intention of living out Mutasina's prophecy. Yes, we'd wiped out Mocri's and Schulz's groups in the prior three days, but we'd also met Hyme's group from *Insectsite* and made friends with them.

Of course, a big part of that was the fact that Hyme was Agil's actual wife, but I wanted to keep working with other *ALO* players and, if possible, folks from other worlds as well. That was why we built Ruis na Ríg.

I got to my feet, washed out the glass pudding container in the kitchen, brushed my teeth at the sink, and headed upstairs to my room.

Once there, I changed into more comfortable clothes, then sent Suguha a text saying I'M DIVING IN FIRST; THERE'S PUDDING IN THE FRIDGE, and went to lie down on the bed. After a moment, I reached up to grab the AmuSphere, put it over my head, and with a breath said, "Link Start."

The falling circle of rainbow light whisked my soul away to another world, where the biggest battle since being converted awaited me.

6

Over half the group was already gathered in the yard outside the log cabin.

Lisbeth was at the smelting furnace, banging away with her hammer, while Sinon watched closely. Asuna and Yui were preparing something at the stove, and Argo and Alice were in conversation near the gate. Agil, Hyme, and Klein were slated to show up around seven o'clock, and the other insects had gone to the Maruba River for some quick leveling, having learned the trick to killing four-eyed giant flatworms from Alice.

Yui was the first to spot me descending the steps of the porch, and she raced right over. "Welcome back, Papa!"

"I'm home, Yui. Thanks for watching the house while I was away," I said, ruffling her hair as she clung to me. She smiled and made a ticklish face. It made me wonder how I was going to ensure her safety during battle.

"Heya. You got enough sleep, Kiri-boy?" Argo smirked, approaching with a jaunty lean, her hands stuck into the pockets of her knickerbockers.

I grimaced and replied, "I bet I did better than you. Sure you don't want to catch a little nap before the operation begins?"

"Wha—? I'm fine, I'm fine. I'd be a poor excuse for an info agent if an all-nighter or two knocked me out."

"Well, I appreciate the effort, but...Hmm? Wait; if you're logged in here, how are you monitoring those social media accounts?"

"Ah, that." Argo peeked down at Yui and beamed. "I know it's cheatin', but I've got Yuicchi keeping tabs on 'em. She's able to monitor social networks while she's online."

"Huh. I see," I murmured, then looked down at Yui, who was still hugging me. "Wait, Yui, are you sure that's safe? It's not going to cause a 'ripple' in your individuality or anything...?"

"No problem!" she claimed, puffing out her chest proudly. "I haven't duplicated my core program; I'm simply multitasking to manage data. Did you know that I am ordinarily maintaining an average of ten thousand tasks in parallel? Adding one more is nothing!"

"T-ten thousand...?"

I couldn't help but stare at her tiny head. Obviously, Yui's brain—her CPU—wasn't contained inside her avatar. Yui's core program was stored on my desktop PC, sitting in my bedroom, but it was so quiet that you wouldn't think it was busy with so many tasks at the same time, and the monthly notice of how much power it was expending didn't add up to all that much.

I loved Yui without reservation, but at the same time, I had no idea what was going on inside her core program. Asking her to show me felt like it would be similar to demanding that Alice show me the lightcube that contained her fluctlight...

Meanwhile, Alice herself walked over and said, "Kirito, if you are rested enough, shall we patrol the nearby woods while waiting for everyone else to arrive?"

"P-patrol? Why?"

"If I were Mutasina, I would send a few scouts first, before the main force leaves. If they are monitoring our actions, then they will know everything we're doing tonight."

"Yeah...I was worried about that, too, so I went out to search the forest last night, but there was no one out there," I told her, glancing toward my partner in that endeavor, Argo, but she just scowled and grumbled.

"Alicchi is right—they could have sent out scouts today, instead. In fact, it would be more natural to assume that…What do the socials look like, Yuicchi?"

Yui blinked, then responded, "Of the twenty-one accounts I am monitoring, eight have been silent for over an hour. The other thirteen have been making increasing statements like 'Getting ready now,' 'Gonna be in all night,' 'The battle is beginning,' and 'Ugh, this sucks.'"

"…I see," said Argo. "Seems like they're just about meetin' up now. Since real-life circumstances come into effect, too, I'm assumin' they won't get all one hundred of the folks who took the Noose, but we should probably assume they'll have at least eighty…no, ninety of 'em…"

"With that many, I would assume five or six scouts would be no problem for them to send. Guess we could go do the rounds again…"

I was wondering whom to choose for this task, looking around the spacious yard area—when the wooden gate swung open, and a cheerful voice boomed, "Hey, guys!"

The *Insectsite* players came stomping through. In the lead was Zarion the rhinoceros beetle, followed by Beeming the stag beetle, then a brown grasshopper. The circular pattern on its forehead was attention-grabbing, but even more curious to me was the white string the grasshopper was dragging behind it.

The string was tied around a long, thin object that was about five and a half feet long. Well, not quite tied—something was wrapped up in the string. Upon a second look, I could see that the object was twitching irregularly.

"……"

I was briefly at a loss for words, but I recovered and approached them, replying in English, "'Sup, guys!" I pointed at the wrapped-up object and asked, "So…what's this?"

The brown grasshopper—technically, a cricket known as *Prosopogryllacris okadai*—named Needy silently lifted the object. Up close, I could see that the white rope was made up of countless extremely thin threads woven together. It looked far sturdier than the crude ropes we were weaving out of grass.

Needy spun the dangling object around. The rope began to unwind around the top of the object, eventually revealing (as I expected) a human being. More specifically, the face of an *ALO* player.

"*Bwaaah!*" gasped the man, taking a deep breath. I took a good look at him; his skin and hair color revealed him to be a salamander, but he was a short and skinny example of one. His bangs were slanted, his eyes were sunken, and he wore a line of pink paint on his left cheek.

When he saw me, he shrieked, "A-are you with these bug people?!"

"Um, yeah."

"Dammit! J-just kill me and get it over with, then!" he raged, which struck me as strange. Something about this situation seemed familiar to me for some reason...

I was about to ask Zarion where they'd caught this man, but someone else behind me shouted, "Ohhh! It's that guy!"

I turned to see Leafa running over, her golden ponytail swinging. She was less than twenty minutes behind me to log in; I thought she'd take much longer. It made me worry that she'd skipped her kendo practice again, but I couldn't ask that and ruin her lively mood. She said hello to the group and approached the strung-up man.

"I knew it...Big B...I mean, Kirito, this is him!"

"Him who?" I asked.

This time it was the man who yelled, "Ahhh! Are you Kirito?! Master Black?!"

"Huh? H-have we met before?"

"It's me! Remember me? On New Year's Day last year, I fought you when you turned all demonic in the Lugru Corridor, and you nearly ate me..."

Two seconds later, I shouted, "Ohhhh! You're that guy!"

*   *   *

It was over a year and a half ago.

Having been freed from the deadly *SAO*, I dived into *ALO* in search of information on Asuna, who should have been logged out but still wasn't waking up. With Leafa and Yui, I headed for the World Tree at the center of the land of fairies. Along the way, we were attacked by a band of salamander mages in a dungeon called the Lugru Corridor, and I managed to fight them off with the very unorthodox method of using spriggan illusion magic to transform into a demon...But if I recalled correctly, Leafa instructed me to take one of them alive and ask why they had attacked.

Back then, too, the man had boldly shouted, "Kill me, if you're going to do it!" but we had ourselves a deal two seconds after I told him I'd offer all the items the deceased salamanders dropped in exchange for the information. Laden with valuables from his dead friends, the man walked off happily, and we never saw him again. Until...

"I dunno...Are you sure...?" I asked, staring at the man in disbelief. But Yui emerged from behind Leafa and stated, "His avatar's appearance and the spectogram of his voiceprint is identical to that of the salamander back then."

"I guess it really is him...What were you doing here, huh?"

"What was I...?" he repeated, his eyes rolling around in stark indecision.

Suddenly struck by an idea, I asked Needy, "Can you loosen the string a bit more?"

Needy's grasshopper face bobbed, and he rotated the dangling man a few more times. Once the rope was slack around his lower jaw, I gave the signal to stop. Sure enough, right around his neck was a black ring-shaped symbol: the Noose of the Accursed.

Meaning that after this salamander had been converted from Alfheim to *Unital Ring*, he joined one of the newly formed cooperative teams and took part in that friendly meetup at the Stiss Ruins.

I considered this knowledge, then said, "Got it. So you got hit by Mutasina's suffocation magic, huh?"

The man's body jerked back and forth. He waggled helplessly in the air and rasped, "Y-you know about her? And this stupid spell she cast?"

"Of course I do. And I know that a hundred players trapped by the Noose just like you are going to attack this town tonight."

At some point, everyone else had gathered around us. Argo was busy interpreting our conversation for the English-speaking insect players.

The man was too stunned to speak, so I took a step closer. "She ordered you to scout out this town, didn't she? Until the insects found you and caught you. And your friends are...?"

I glanced over at Zarion and Beeming. The rhinoceros beetle and stag beetle just shrugged the moment Argo's translation caught up.

"...Guess they fought back and died. So what will you do? You know we can't just release you. Will you bounce out of *Unital Ring* now, or will you be our prisoner and tell us what you know?" I said, presenting him with his options in as stern and menacing a tone as I could muster.

The man studiously avoided looking me in the eyes again, until he finally summoned up some guts and stared me back in the face. "Kirito, you know how freakin' scary the Noose's effect is—and you still want to fight Mutasina? You'd be better off not taking her magic lightly. You can't just withstand the effect with willpower and mental preparation. I don't wanna be her slave either, but the only way to survive in *UR* is to obey her..."

I lifted my hand to stop him from speaking further. I grabbed the throat protector of my armor and pulled it down, along with my undershirt. His eyes and mouth went wide, and he fell silent.

"Kirito," whispered Asuna nervously. Her concern was well-founded. It was utterly reckless to reveal to him that I was under the effect of the Noose. If he told Mutasina about that, she could shut me down with a single thump of her staff before my sword could reach her.

Which made this a gamble. If I could get the information this man knew, we could improve the chances of our plan working. In order to do that, I'd need to convince him that there was a chance he could be freed from the suffocation spell.

The man wasn't saying anything yet, so I tried the last resort.

"If you tell us everything you know, and we beat Mutasina in battle tonight, I'll give you everything she drops. Except for the staff—I'm breaking that, of course."

He exhaled, long and slow, then smiled weakly and asked, "Really?"

When the salamander named Friscoll was freed from Needy's strings, he plopped himself down in the middle of the open plaza and demanded something to drink.

Asuna offered him some lukewarm tea. He drank three cups *and* chowed down on some harve meat stew to boot. In the meantime, I asked Zarion what had happened.

The insects had taken a break from hunting four-eyed giant flatworms and decided to return to Ruis na Ríg to recover SP, until Harvey the *Anaciaeschna martini* dragonfly, who had excellent eyesight, spotted four players hiding in the brush. The insects split into two groups and approached, but the hiding players attacked before they could talk to them, and so they had to defeat three of the four, then captured Friscoll when he tried to flee and brought him back to Ruis na Ríg with them. The white rope that tied him up wasn't crafted out of material items but was part of a skill Needy had to produce the silk from his mouth.

In the real world, such crickets could indeed produce silk. That made me wonder if most of these insect avatars could actually fly, but like the *ALO* players, their ability of flight had been removed. It seemed like a major disadvantage to insects like dragonflies and bees, which were known for flying, but according to them, even in *Insectsite*, flight was held to very limited distances. As

Zarion told me with great chagrin, that was because in the very early days of the game, certain idiotic players would log out and then try to jump down their stairs and get hurt.

In any case, with the help of Alice's flatworm-hunting method, the *Insectsite* team reached an average level of 15. They were below the *ALO* players, but they would still be much higher than Mutasina's army, which was only leveling around the starting ruins. Unfortunately, it wasn't going to be enough of a difference to make up for the gap in personnel numbers, but we were going to get to the bottom of that soon.

Once Friscoll's SP and TP were recovered, the questioning fell to Argo, who worked as a writer and researcher in real life. The Rat used clever lines of inquiry to trap Friscoll in various webs, and we had a great deal of information in just fifteen minutes.

According to the interrogation, Mutasina's army's average level was around 10 or 11, and they were leaving at nine o'clock, later than our initial expectations. As we predicted, they would be traveling along the east bank of the Maruba River and expected to arrive at Ruis na Ríg exactly at midnight. Again, as we predicted, their strategy was to destroy the forest around the town to create a flat, open area. If we hid in the town, they would use the logs to break down the wall, and if we charged them, they'd surround us and allow Mutasina to cast the Noose on us.

Excluding the four scouts in the party, their total group was eighty-seven in number, with those players who couldn't attend due to real-life scheduling being left out of any distribution of spoils and reward payment.

"What's the reward payment?" Lisbeth asked.

Friscoll made a face that suggested he wasn't sure what to think. "They say it's ten el per person, but I dunno. That's a thousand el, if it goes to a hundred people. All the materials I gathered in an entire day added up to less than thirty dim. How did Mutasina and the VSS save up a thousand el with just the four of them? It's impossible."

The VSS was presumably her club, the Virtual Study Society.

I didn't know there were only four members. This would mean that the other three in the club knew about the effect of the Noose but accepted its effects in the big coliseum roundup in order to help pull the spell off—and had to withstand the choking demonstration.

"...What are the other three in the VSS like?" I asked.

Friscoll made a face. "Hmm...I dunno; it's hard to say much about 'em. There are two swordswomen with almost identical faces and builds called Viola and Dia—and a dark mage guy named Magis. They're basically like the lieutenants of the group. The two women won't chat with you at all, and the mage is actually pretty decent once you talk to him, but...I dunno how to describe it..."

He grimaced, clearly wanting to say something but not finding the right words to describe it. Eventually, he gave up and shrugged.

"Anyway, they're all weird, including Mutasina. If they're that tough from the very start, they'd have to be absolute top-tier players in *ALO*, but nobody's ever seen them before or heard their names. Do they ring a bell to you?" he asked.

We shared a look. It was indeed just as he'd said—no recognition, just silent headshaking.

"...Is it possible that they're aliases? The player's cursor doesn't show up here until you attack or get attacked, you know. When she cast the Noose on me, she was too far away to see her cursor well," I pointed out.

Friscoll performed a two-finger spinning gesture in the air. "There's another way to see a player's name aside from their cursor, you know. I've been in a raid party with the other three, so I made to sure to check on their names that appear up here on the left. That's how I know how to spell the three names. If you ask me, they sound pretty typical for player names."

I looked to Yui, not recognizing those names, but even she shook her head—she would remember every individual we'd come into contact with in Alfheim.

Not only did we not find their identities, we were left with more mysteries than before. But…

"In any case, this doesn't change what we need to do. We'll beat Mutasina and clear up this hurdle before we head off for the center of the world. It's been a long series of events since that first night, but this time, we're going to get a good clean start for ourselves!" I announced, rousing my companions. Everyone gathering in the yard in front of the log cabin—even Friscoll, shamelessly—lifted a fist into the air and roared in response.

Agil, Hyme, and Klein showed up at the time they mentioned, maxing out our group. We discussed a number of issues first, then left Ruis na Ríg at eight o'clock.

The first issue was what to do with Friscoll, who was technically our prisoner. It was impossible for me to see his reactions after being dragged in by Zarion's group as anything but natural, but there was always the possibility that he was acting as a double agent, pretending to give us info and leaking ours to Mutasina's side. If this were Aincrad, we could lock him up in a room somewhere, but in *Unital Ring*, you could always log out, and then we couldn't stop him from making contact with his friends in the real world. Friscoll's three companions had surely alerted Mutasina's army that they'd already died by now.

After much discussion without including the man in question, we decided that we would be taking Friscoll with us. Despite being a rather inhumane line of action, we wrapped him back up in Needy's threads before starting our preparations for the battle and dangled him from a tree. Without being able to use his hands, he couldn't bring up the menu or log out. If his heart rate or need to urinate rose above the base levels, the AmuSphere would automatically cut him off, and if he didn't return within several minutes, we'd know that he had betrayed us. We did offer him two options of either being tied up and traveling with us or being monitored in the Bashin home area, where they'd cut off his head if he opened his menu. Scowling, he chose the former.

The second issue was what to do about the Bashin and the Patter.

Personally, I wanted to avoid any NPC casualties at all, so I preferred for them to stay at Ruis na Ríg, but both groups stubbornly insisted that it was their home now, too, and they demanded to fight to protect it. As a compromise, we took five warriors from each group with us. Naturally, among them were Yzelma, leader of the Bashin, and Chett, leader of the Patter—both women, coincidentally—along with four of their handpicked best.

That put our number in the battle party at eleven of us, twenty of Hyme and her friends, and ten NPCs: forty-one in total. Plus Misha, Kuro, Aga, and Pina.

At eight thirty, we arrived at the spot that Argo and I picked out the night before. First, we strung up Friscoll from a tree a ways from the river, then used the resources we'd packed into all of our item storage—aside from the NPCs'—to start building the contraption that would form the essence of our counterplan. It was the kind of massive construction that would take a month with heavy equipment in the real world, but as long as you understood the tricks of the crafting system, you could build it all with the proper hand gestures in this world.

Despite struggling a little with the fine-tuning, we were finished by nine thirty. Now all we had to do was wait for Mutasina's army.

The enemy was supposedly leaving the Stiss Ruins at nine, so I would have liked to send out scouts of our own to check on their location, but there was no guarantee we wouldn't get spotted and caught like Friscoll's group had.

It was possible they might change their route just beforehand, but if they didn't pass through the safe Maruba River, that would mean cutting through the Zelletelio Forest in the middle of the night. There were almost no dangerous monsters in the southern portion, but that was because we were at an average of level-15, and even the frequent bats and foxes were much more dangerous than the tiny critters that populated the Stiss Ruins region.

According to Friscoll, Mutasina's army had no better than leather armor, so if they just so happened across a large creature like a thornspike cave bear, even a huge battalion of ninety or so was going to suffer 10 or 20 percent losses. We knew that Mutasina's strategy was to surround us with a superior force to hold us in place, so she'd want to avoid losing any of them before they could execute their plan.

Their main advantage was the size of their army. To make use of it, they absolutely needed a large open space. That meant they had to travel north up the Maruba River.

I watched our completed defenses beginning to work and pondered the probabilities of the various ways this could all play out.

Yui approached me and looked up. "I'm sorry, Papa..."

"Hm...? For what?"

"If I were still a navigation pixie, I could access the map data and confirm the route the enemy is taking to approach...," she said, crestfallen.

I knelt down to look her in the eyes, then put my arms around her. "I'm glad you're a player now, Yui," I whispered. "Yes, I'm worried that you're no longer impervious to damage...But this means there are so many more things we can share, right? I know I've had you deciphering NPC language and monitoring social media, but those are things you're doing with your own talent; you're not accessing the game system behind the scenes to do them. So, uh..."

I ran out of steam and wasn't sure how to continue. Fortunately, there was a gentle voice overhead to pick up where I left off:

"You're our child, Yui, so you don't have to push yourself so hard," said Asuna, who knelt beside me and caressed Yui's head. The girl reached out with one hand, still cradled in my embrace, and grabbed Asuna's dress.

"Mama..."

"Of course, we're very happy to see you trying so hard, but now that you're finally a player like us, we want you to enjoy your life in this world. I know it sounds silly to say this, when we're about to have a war…But one part of the fun in a game is the chance to pit yourself against a worthy opponent."

Something in her gentle voice caused my eyes to bolt wide open. Ever since being put under the Noose of the Accursed in the ruins, I'd been trying to gauge the depth of Mutasina's evil. I was so focused on the "darkness" she spoke about that I never tried to examine the darkness within me.

But taking a step back and trying to be objective, Mutasina was just another player in the game called *Unital Ring*. The sudden-death rules of this game were harsh, but unlike in Aincrad, nobody was going to lose their life here. What was about to happen was a huge PvP battle but not an actual, bloody slaughter…

I rearranged my arms so I had one around Yui and the other around Asuna and squeezed them both. "Yeah. Let's do our best…and enjoy this," I whispered. "Even if we lose, it's only happening in a game. We can always get back what we've lost. All you need to do is what you've been doing already as a player, Yui."

Trapped between our chests, Yui gave a muffled but determined "I will!"

Kuro, who had been lying down nearby, promptly growled in apparent agreement. I looked over at the creature and noticed that our friends were watching the three of us with big grins.

At eleven, everyone was at their stations. All members were registered in a raid party, aside from the Bashin and the Patter. All preparations were complete.

At eleven thirty, Sinon, who was monitoring downriver through the Hecate II's scope, sent a message that said, *I see light that looks like torches.*

At eleven forty-five, while hiding in the brush, I spotted the flickering orange light, too.

7

The sound of an army of boots scraping against the gravel of the riverbank echoed heavily in the dark of night.

It was a raiding party of nearly ninety, and despite being cobbled together from players threatened into line, there was not a single idle comment from the group. They had originally come together for the purpose of conquering *Unital Ring*, so their discipline was better than I'd given them credit for.

But our morale was just as high, if not higher. Between the *ALO* and *Insectsite* players, we presented a more motley collection, but the forty-four of us lurked in total silence among the woods on both sides of the Maruba. I couldn't even hear anyone breathing.

Mutasina's group was traveling along the wide east bank of the river at a measured pace. I could make out not just their torchlight, but also the dull gleam of the flames' light reflecting off their leather armor.

The real issue was where in the line Mutasina was. We couldn't activate the trap until we'd identified her location. Currently, the Kirito Army—I had no choice but to begrudgingly accept the name—was split into two groups hiding in the trees on either side of the river. I was in charge of the eastern team, while Asuna led the western team. Only Asuna, Sinon, and I, waiting far upriver, had our ring menus open so we could send a friend message to the other two as soon as we spotted Mutasina, alerting them to her location. So far there had been no word from the other two.

The reason only the three of us had our menus open was because the light of the windows threatened to give away our hiding spots. The three of us were each hiding in brush covered by a thick, light-blocking black cloth. If we had more of that cloth, we could have more players with their windows open, but Asuna hadn't developed black dye yet. We had repurposed the fabric from black clothing dropped by deceased players.

I stared at the riverbed through a narrow gap in the cloth. The lead torch swaying at the front of the group was under sixty feet away now, and I could clearly see the players.

The front line was made up of tanks, equipped with studded leather armor and round leather shields. Their large bodies and shields were blocking my view of those behind them. I'd have to wait for the first group to pass to search for Mutasina, but being only three feet higher in the woods than along the river, we invited a higher chance of being spotted the longer we waited here.

Just to my right, Kuro's sinuous body tensed. I ran a gentle hand down its back, mentally willing the panther to stay calm. Misha was also on the east bank, while Aga was waiting with Asuna on the west bank. We'd just have to pray that all three beasts stayed quiet.

The three tanks in the front row passed by, just fifteen feet away. I recognized the middle of the three, who was especially tall. He was the leader of the Absolute Survivor Squad who'd put together the meetup at the Stiss Ruins: Holgar. He played a cheerful MC onstage, but the look on his face as he walked past was tense and determined.

The studded armor on the tanks was heavy as far as leather was concerned, but they had no throat guards, so their necks were clearly visible. I could see the black rings clearly by the orange light of the torches.

Mutasina said that cursed noose was what would bind the *ALO* players together and guide them to the final destination. But that wasn't going to be the end of the game. Where was the fun in playing a game where you carried out orders due to nothing but the terror of suffocation?

I wasn't crying foul over Mutasina's play style. She was just taking the best option available to her as one of many players trapped in *Unital Ring*. And we were doing everything we could to compete with her, too.

Once Holgar and the other tanks had passed, the next group was the lightly armored scouts, dressed in cloth armor and bearing short swords and daggers. No sign of Mutasina yet. Could she be elsewhere? But then you would expect these players to at least chat a little. No, the witch had to be somewhere among the ranks.

Where? Where could she be?

In less than three minutes, the head of the procession would reach the trap. Whatever the case, we had to activate it at that moment. But once it happened, our chances of stopping Mutasina dropped drastically.

Sinon had to be feeling extremely frustrated upriver. I wanted to send her a reassuring message of patience, but I couldn't spare the attention. I kept my eyes open as wide as I could, staring carefully at the silent army before me.

Night Vision proficiency has risen to 7, said a sudden pop-up window, blocking my sight. I swept it aside, trying to keep my irritation in check.

At that very moment, a silhouette firmly lodged in my memory came into view: a long staff, rising from the center of the group of attackers equipped with leather armor and longswords.

A staff with a huge gemstone embedded into its diamond-shaped head—held by a slender player wearing a white robe with the hood pulled low. That could be none other than Mutasina the witch.

There were two shorter swordsmen in front of Mutasina. Their blackish armor, done in the same style, looked quite expensive for being leather. They wore hats of similar material, and I couldn't make out their faces, but I presumed that was Viola and Dia, like Friscoll had told us.

And behind her was a tall mage wearing a pitch-black robe. The mage's staff was quite long but otherwise unremarkable. That had to be the dark mage named Magis. So those four were the entirety of the Virtual Study Society.

Two swordsmen and two mages was a good grouping for a quartet, but it seemed unbalanced to have both spellcasters be dark mages. Presumably, they had inherited the dark magic skill from *ALO*, but in *Unital Ring*, magic skills started off locked, and you could only activate them by finding and using a magicrystal of that type. Those were rare enough to begin with; where had they found two crystals, both darkness-type?

I really wanted to find out, but I knew I wouldn't have the chance to ask. In no more than ten minutes, either Mutasina or I would be dead.

She was coming closer and closer, surrounded by swordsmen like her personal guard. Despite the fist-sized rocks all over the riverbank, her avatar's upper half stayed almost perfectly still. The other three were the same way…They were extremely used to the full-dive environment. That would mean their senses were proportionately sharp. The moment they were closest to me would be the moment our ambush was most in danger of being exposed.

They were approaching directly, their pace undisturbed. They got closer and closer to the brush where I was hiding…and then passed, heading upriver. Holgar's front line was already lost in the darkness behind me.

Ahead of their march was a small waterfall about six feet tall, which splashed cheerily. Naturally, the riverbank was blocked off by a steep slope the same height, but the ground was worn away in steps, so even the heavily armored soldiers would be able to get up without trouble.

However, they would not be climbing the slope and proceeding upriver.

The falls rushing over the slope here did not exist two and a half hours ago. We chose a spot where the woods encroached on the water from both sides and then worked together with tons of logs and stone to back up the river, creating an impromptu dam.

I got the hint for this idea when returning from the Stiss Ruins two nights ago, when I used the crafting system to block the entrance to the cave behind the waterfall. I assumed that it would be impossible, but Argo's insistence that this game was challenging its players' common gaming wisdom turned into a new perspective for me.

In *Unital Ring*, players had greater freedom than in *SAO* or *ALO*. That included the freedom to change the landscape to a degree. You couldn't abruptly block off a river with a wall of stone, but if you gave the flowing water a new place to run, it was eminently possible to craft objects within the flow.

First, I stuck sturdy logs into the fifteen-foot-wide river, about three feet apart. Between the logs, I stuck not stone walls, but one-foot stone barriers, slowly and methodically raising the barrier each time.

From upriver, it was obvious that it was an artificial object blocking the flow of the river. But from downriver, the falls where the river spilled over the dam hid it from view. Even farther still, I'd gone down a huge waterfall a hundred feet tall with Alice and Argo in the canoe, so surely the presence of six-foot falls here wouldn't seem unnatural. Sure enough, the lead of the procession wasn't stopping. They marched right up to the stair-shaped slope on the right side of the falls. Mutasina was not giving the order to halt.

I could practically feel the prickling nerves of my companions, lying in wait. Every one of them had to be thinking, *Hurry, hurry.* But not quite…We needed Mutasina's group to get as close to the falls as possible, or they would be able to rush up the side of the bank to safety.

Just a little closer…Three more feet………

Now.

I hit the SEND button on the message written up in my window.

The simple command *FIRE!* traveled to Asuna and Sinon at once.

Half a second later, a massive hole appeared in the middle of the fifteen-foot-wide falls, and a pillar of water shot up from the river surface in front of it. Almost as quickly after that, a roar like thunder filled the air.

"Whoa!!"

"Was that lightning?!"

Mutasina's army was suddenly out of order, players speaking up in alarm. But the real shock was only just starting.

There were five pillars holding up our dam. The four on the left and right were made from good old spiral pine, but the one in the center was rarer, stronger Zelle teak.

The log that had withstood the incredible water pressure against the dam for two and a half hours had just shattered spectacularly, courtesy of a 12.7 mm bullet from Sinon's Hecate II. One of her six precious bullets remaining, probably never to be replaced.

At our meeting at the log cabin, we naturally considered using the Hecate to snipe Mutasina herself. But the inherited weapon was a true monster, equivalent to my Excalibur or even greater, and demanded stats to match it. In her current state, Sinon couldn't equip it. Klein suggested creating a transportable rifle stand, and Agil offered to carry it himself, but neither plan would make precision firing possible.

Instead, I suggested fixing the Hecate tight to some logs, preventing any aim adjustment but allowing it to fire at one precise point. Our aim would be pointed not at a player, but at the Zelle teak log holding up the dam.

A direct hit from a bullet that would probably kill the Life Harvester in one shot proved to be more than enough to shatter the twenty-inch-thick log. As for what happened after that...

With a tremendous roar load enough to wipe away any trace of the memory of the gunshot a second earlier, the dam crumbled from the center without its core support.

A deluge of water, littered with shards of stone and wood, was fully unleashed. The front line of Mutasina's army was swallowed up without a prayer of escape. Even a heavily armored warrior couldn't withstand the pent-up energy of water held behind a dam for two and a half hours. A number of them tried to cross the flow to climb the banks, but they never got close, screaming as the turgid maelstrom overwhelmed them.

As the chaos unfolded, I watched the center of the formation very closely.

In impressive fashion, the four members of the Virtual Study Society did not succumb to panic in the face of the flash flood. Mutasina did come to a stop, but the swordswomen in black, Viola and Dia, shouted in unison, "Everyone, climb the bank!"

They moved to evacuate to the east of the river—toward the woods where we lurked—but having dozens of damage dealers crowded in such tight formation backfired on them. The tanks and scouts, swept backward by the rush, collided with the damage dealers, tangling up with them and creating a huge obstacle.

Mutasina's quartet was still for one moment, then swallowed up by water. Whether calm or panicked, no player could stand their ground against the flood.

As soon as I had visual confirmation that her group was flushed, I sent the next message.

GO!

This one was for Asuna, although I sent it to Sinon as well. Together, we leaped from the undergrowth and gave hand signals to our parties lying in wait nearby.

With Kuro very slightly in the lead, I ran at a full sprint on the boundary right between the forest and riverbed. Even at full speed, I could just barely catch up to Mutasina's group in the water. Perhaps some of the players noticed us, but trapped in the rapids as they were, it was all they could do just to keep from drowning.

As I ran, the force of the rushing water gradually weakened. First, the heavily armored players snagged on rocks or branches on the river floor, then the mid-tier players tangled up with them. At the head of the lightly armored players, still floating on the surface, were Magis and Mutasina, who had to be the lightest of all in terms of equipment weight. They'd been pulled away from Viola and Dia.

So far, everything had gone to plan. Now we just had to wait for Mutasina to stop. I was worried about Magis being so close, but a mage wouldn't be able to react quickly to a rush attack.

The level of the surge was growing lower. Even the light-armor players were getting stuck now, clambering up onto the shore of their own power. Ahead of Mutasina and Magis, who were still rushing along, was a large sandbank. They course corrected to head for it, jabbing the ends of their staffs into the gravelly front end of the sandbank...and stopping.

This was it.

"Let's go!" I shouted tersely, and I burst out from the woods, jumping down to the riverbed three feet below. As soon as I landed, my sword was free, and I was running full-bore at Mutasina, who was less than sixty feet ahead. The river flowed between the riverbed and sandbank, but because it was being diverted around that bank, the flow was less than fifteen feet wide, and I could leap over it with the help of a sword skill.

On the far side of the river, Asuna's team jumped down at the same time, sprinting forward. I could hear the cries and roars of the light-armor units farther upriver as they spotted us, but I had Misha leading a separate group to deal with them.

My job was to remove Mutasina from *Unital Ring* forever. Going for the kill without mercy did not really resonate with my personal ethos, but I knew from the moment she put the symbol around my throat that she would not compromise through dialogue. Freeing the shackled players and preventing my friends from suffering the same fate required me to do the mission like this, right now.

At the tip of the sandbar, Mutasina and Magis were finally getting up, having noticed our ambush, but their movements were awkward, either from dizziness at being tossed about by the water or because their waterlogged robes were too heavy. Even if they tried to use magic, I could stop their gestures with a sword skill at this distance.

I rested my sword on my right shoulder, prepping for the Sonic Leap skill.

Three steps until I was in range. Two...

Suddenly, the riverbed beneath my feet glowed bluish-purple.

And not just that. There were curves, patterns, and symbols appearing on the rocky surface in a complex texture. It was a magic circle. In fact...

It was the precursor effect to the Noose of the Accursed spell.

The vast circle, 150 feet across, completely spanned both my team and Asuna's. But why? Mutasina was right in front of me, using her staff to prop herself up. She wasn't making the activation gesture. The same was true of Magis.

But the last thing I should do was stand around being shocked. I was already under the Noose's effects, but I couldn't let the same happen to my friends.

Behind the stunned witch, a monster arose that looked like nothing but some horrible god. It had the torso of a woman, sitting atop a writhing mass of tentacles. Its four arms had two joints each, and its head was all bristling spikes.

"Everyone, get out of the magic circle!! You too, Kuro!!" I shouted as loudly as I could, activating Sonic Leap. I didn't know how they activated the spell, but as long as I defeated Mutasina, the Noose would be dispelled permanently, even if the others couldn't escape in time.

"Haah!"

I launched myself off the ground the moment I sensed the system acceleration kicking in, crossing the fifteen feet of river in a single bound and slashing at Mutasina's helpless, unprotected shoulder.

Kachiiiing! There was a tremendous clatter, and a hard shock ran through my arm, numbing up to my elbow. Behind Mutasina, Magis had stuck out his staff with frightening speed—and his weapon, which looked for all the world like a gnarled tree branch, stopped my sword. The steel blade sank several inches into the head of the staff, but his weapon was clearly finer than it looked, because it stopped my attack cold.

The force of the sword skill dispersed from there, blowing back Mutasina's hood with a gust of wind. Jet-black long hair whipped violently, and the light of the magic circle revealed a pale face.

Her features were fine and beautiful, just as I recalled. But there was a sharp pang in my mind, a needle of *wrongness*. The source was…her eyes. Though there was no emotion in her face, there was a patina of fright in her wide gray eyes. The Mutasina I saw in the ruins would not have been alarmed in the least, even with the tip of a sword a hairbreadth from her eyeball.

This was someone else. A body double.

My moment of realization coincided with beams of light shooting from all four of the monster's arms.

Greeeee!

The beams shrieked like a monster, striking all my companions as they attempted to escape the circle. Unfortunately, I had to assume that no one had enough time to get away. Even the body double before me buckled as the beam struck her exposed throat. Once enough beams had shot out for everyone present, the monstrosity crumbled into nothingness.

Mutasina was somewhere nearby and had arranged for a body double with an identical staff, just to lure us into the range of her Noose—and then cast the suffocation spell on everyone, without mercy. I recalled now that Mutasina had included the members of the Virtual Study Society at the meeting at the Stiss Ruins in order to win the trust of the others—and swept them all up in it. Her companions probably agreed to be part of the lure, and it was a clever plan, no doubt about it—but it made me sick to think about.

With my sword still trapped in Magis's staff, I asked the unfamiliar body double, "Is this really what you want?"

It was not she who answered, but Magis, who loomed behind her back like a reaper.

"Good grief," he exclaimed, from the darkness of his hood. "Listen, Kirito. I'm not denying your right to pursue your heroic ideals, but we're doing our best to beat this game here. Is this really the place for pushing your standards on others?"

His voice was deep and soft, like a teacher's, but his words were sharp. Yes, everyone had a right to play an MMORPG in their own way, and you couldn't lecture others on how they should follow your own moral superiority. In fact, it wasn't just his voice and tone—even his point sounded teacherly...

Suddenly, it struck me:

This was "Sensei." He was the mystery person who taught Mocri's party how to fight other players—and possibly instigated Schulz's group into making their attack. If so, then even this unnecessary conversation was probably masking some strategic purpose of his.

Mutasina had already achieved her goal of casting the Noose on us; all she had to do was activate the effect to bend all of us to her will. All she had to do was bang the butt of her staff against the ground, so why wasn't she doing it?

Can she not do it yet? Is she in some place where she can't?

Maybe it was a place without solid ground. Like the river. Or... "The sky!"

I pushed forward with my sword for all I was worth and looked at the sky.

Although there was no moon, the stars were out. By opening my eyes for all they were worth, my Night Vision effect kicked in, brightening the details a little. Against the dark-gray sky was a black shape, circling silently. It was a huge bird with a wingspan of at least ten feet. I couldn't see from the ground, but most likely Mutasina was on its back. Perhaps it was circling because it was looking for a safe place to land in the forest.

Once she landed, that would be checkmate. We had to do something while she was still airborne. But I couldn't reach her with a sword skill, and the only ranged attacks we had were Yui's fire magic, my decay magic, and Sinon's Hecate. With the sniper rifle's aim fixed in place, that was out; and the Flame Arrow starting spell wasn't going to be strong enough to take down that giant bird. My Rotten Shot spell wouldn't be much more than a nasty prank.

I briefly glanced upstream, where the enemy forces swept up in the flash flood were starting to recover. Once they recognized the situation, they would follow their initial orders and attack us. It wasn't clear if the lieutenants would stop them, but we couldn't just let things play out like this.

About the only option left was to pick up a rock and throw it. I started thinking frantically in that direction when a ferocious roar erupted from behind me.

"Groaaaahh!"

Standing on two legs on the riverbank was Misha the thorn-spike cave bear, both paws extended to their full length. The zig-zagging white pattern on its chest glowed in the faint starlight.

That was right—we did have *one* ranged attack.

Misha's chest pattern flashed. The plethora of needles that shot from it sped through the night sky like antiair missiles, enveloping the huge bird that was circling nearly two hundred feet overhead. Feathers exploded without a sound.

It did not succeed at eliminating all of the bird's HP, but it did cause the creature to lose its balance. The bird started to plummet toward the ground, beating its wings frantically to regain lift.

That was bad. Mutasina still had the option of simply fleeing the area. If she pulled the bird away and out of sight, we'd never get another chance to kill her.

Fall! Please fall! I willed.

Then another burst of feathers fell from the bird's right breast. I heard a gunshot resound: *Baaang...*It was not the rumbling boom of the Hecate. Sinon must have left her position to come closer, then shot at the bird with a musket.

The added damage was too much for the monstrous bird to withstand this time. It clumsily flapped its wings and began to descend toward the river. As it flew lower, the figure on the bird's back came into view.

Mutasina had avoided the needles' direct blast, but she had no choice of landing spots now. Could I defeat her the instant she came down? That would determine the outcome of this battle.

I let the tension go out of my knees and sank without warning. My sword, still sunk into Magis's staff, pulled back above my right shoulder. With a very slight adjustment in my stance, the blade began to glow blue. When you couldn't move your sword, you could move your body to force it into the proper motion for a sword skill.

"Mmm...?" Magis grunted. He tried to leap away, but it was too late.

Pushing the stunned body double out of the way with my free hand, I activated the single-hit Vertical skill with my sword arm.

Shunk! The blade cut through both the long staff and the fingers of the man holding it. Now the mage could not perform any magic spell gestures until he recovered from the localized damage. I would have liked to finish him off right away, but there were more pressing matters.

"Everyone, aim for the spot where the bird falls!" I shouted, leaping over the fallen Magis and launching into a sprint.

I prayed that she would fall somewhere without any impediments downriver, but of course it wasn't going to be that convenient. The nose-diving bird was going to crash onto the west side of the river, about twenty yards upstream of the sandbank.

Mutasina's forces were bristling along the right edge of the water, but they either weren't recovered from the shock of the flash flood yet or were intimidated by Misha's roar; they were reacting slowly. I would probably still have a chance to get one good hit in on Mutasina after she landed.

I crossed the water with a normal jump this time, over to the west bank. On my left, I was joined by Asuna, her rapier drawn.

A moment's glance in her direction was enough to spot the dark ring around her slender throat. But there wasn't a shred of fear in her features. There was only pure concentration in her eyes as she raced for our destination, fully inhabiting the Flash identity once more.

Mutasina's mount was a bird of prey with dark feathers. I couldn't tell if it was an eagle or a hawk, but its sharp talons and beak would surely pack a nasty punch. For now, however, it was all it could do to slow down its falling speed, so I didn't feel the need to count it as an enemy. My only target was Mutasina. I would cut her in two the moment she jumped off the bird's back and descended to the ground.

As I ran, I measured the timing for my sword skill.

In the back of my head, I envisioned what would happen in several seconds. Mutasina would jump off the giant bird's back just before it slammed into the riverbank, land, and jam her staff into the ground. I started a mental countdown until the time I'd need to let the Sonic Leap fly, so that I hit her at the same time she landed. Seven, six, five…

Just then, a small figure separated from the falling bird. Mutasina had leaped off.

"…!!"

I held my breath as I ran. She was still at least seventy feet up in the air. There was no way she could land steadily from a height like that. She would suffer huge damage in that fall, unless she'd taken the Landing ability in the Swiftness tree and raised it up to a rank of 10.

Or maybe she had some other method of neutralizing her speed—but Mutasina fell to earth even faster than the bird. Rather than spreading her limbs in an attempt to increase wind resistance, she straightened herself out, jutting the staff in her right hand forward toward the ground.

Suddenly, I realized what she was planning to do. Nearby, Asuna gasped.

"Rgh…"

We picked up our speed. I went into the windup motion for Sonic Leap, while Asuna did the same for Shooting Star. Light infused my longsword and her rapier, and they began to vibrate with high-pitched whines…But before I could launch myself forward, the butt of Mutasina's staff made contact with a large rock on the riverbank.

Craaaaack! With a sound like a gunshot, the stone split in two.

Mutasina's hand let go of the staff. She hit the bank shoulder-first, bounced violently, did a somersault, and fell to the ground.

The sigil around our necks—the Noose of the Accursed—began to glow a blue-purple color.

Something sticky blocked my windpipe. I couldn't breathe in or out. It was that realistic sense of suffocation, the thing I never wanted to experience again.

Ignore it! This is an illusion! I told myself with all the willpower I had, activating Sonic Leap. While Asuna's attempt stumbled somewhat, she also succeeded at executing a Shooting Star.

Up ahead, the witch in the white robe was lifting herself up. The Noose must have counted as an attack, but her spindle cursor was active over her head. While jabbing the rock with the staff had countered some of the shock of impact, her hit points were still at no more than 20 percent.

Either attack of ours would be enough to finish her off, if they hit her.

"……!!" I roared silently, swinging the glowing green sword right down toward Mutasina's left shoulder.

The deadly sword tip lunged toward the downcast witch—and then, with phenomenal speed, a dark shadow darted before me and deflected my attack with a slender longsword. Next to me, Asuna's rapier was handled by another shadow. Two metallic clashes rang out, and orange sparks illuminated the figures.

They were both short women dressed in black leather armor, wearing leather hats of the same color. It was Viola and Dia of the Virtual Study Society. My foe glared at me with fearsome glee and hostility. There was a glowing ring around her narrow neck. Neither of them could breathe, either, but they'd leaped out of the river to defend Mutasina.

The glowing light on my sword and Asuna's guttered out.

At the same time, the pain in my throat reached its peak, and I fell to my knees. Asuna, too, crumbled on my left. I wanted to help her escape, at the least, but then Viola and Dia fell to the ground, too. Despite knowing about the effect of the spell, the Virtual Study Society members could not withstand its agony, either.

I couldn't blame them. Even knowing that your real body was still perfectly fine, the sensation of being unable to breathe summoned a primordial fear that numbed the limbs and sapped your ability to think. My heart raced, and the blood pumped tirelessly in my ears.

Straining to look behind me, I could see all our companions kneeling on the riverbed or fallen to the ground. The Bashin, the Patter, and even the pets were included. It was difficult to watch Kuro, Aga, and Misha curled up in agony, the Noose shining around their necks.

On the right, nearly a hundred players had fallen back into the water, struggling mightily. No one could speak, so the only sounds were the rushing of the water and the weak beating of the giant bird's injured wings, now that it, too, had landed on the riverbed.

In the midst of this quiet hell, the witch slowly rose to her feet.

She squeezed the staff, still stuck between the pieces of the rock, and pulled it out of the ground. The gemstone embedded in the head was glowing the same eerie blue-purple color as the Noose.

Mutasina swept her hood back, revealing her beauty, and surveyed the area. Her facial features were indeed similar to the body double's, but there was something faintly inhuman about the air of the real thing.

Facing forward once more, her thin lips curved into a hint of a smile.

"Splendidly done," she murmured, walking up to Asuna and me. She stopped just behind the struggling Viola and Dia and

continued, "I had a feeling you would not be so boring as to hide in your base…But I never expected you to dam the river. I'd no idea the crafting system could perform feats like that. Your plan completely surpassed my expectations. I assumed that I would not take more than a tenth of my health in damage all the way to the end of the game, but you nearly killed me by forcing me to jump from my flying mount."

She chuckled gleefully, and her face blurred into two, then united again. Was it a visual artifact of the Noose, or was it because my biological brain was surging with adrenaline? I could beat Mutasina if I could just slice her now, but there was no strength with which I could hold my sword. Against the panic of the suffocation, it was all I could do to keep my body still.

Asuna had her left hand to her throat, with her right stuck into the sand of the riverbank. The sight of her brought me a fresh wave of fury at the woman before me, but even that was overwhelmed by the horrible inability to breathe.

I had believed that, despite whatever horrible magic Mutasina possessed, she was still nothing but another *Unital Ring* player. That her cruel methods and mannerisms were simply her particular play style. But I was naive. This woman wasn't an ordinary person playing the role of the evil witch. She was challenging this world not as a VRMMO gamer, but as something from another dimension entirely.

As though sensing the horror coursing through my mind, she said, "So are you reaching your limit? When I tested this before, no one could break through the three-minute barrier. There is only one way to escape the Noose: to log out. Of course, that will leave your avatar right here, entirely helpless."

She waved the butt of the long staff in the air teasingly. If we could get her to hit the ground with it, the agony would end.

Suddenly, Mutasina's smile vanished. With a detached expression, she stared down at me and announced, "Kirito the Black Swordsman. Asuna the Flash. If you would swear loyalty to me in exchange for the end of your suffering, offer your sword hilts."

In game terms, this was utterly meaningless. If I offered her my sword, I would have plenty of chances to take Mutasina by surprise and ambush her later.

But neither I, nor Asuna, nor any of our companions (I suspected) had the personality...or the beliefs that would allow this. If we pledged loyalty in exchange for our lives, we would have no choice but to play out that choice. Mutasina was demanding an oath on my sword, knowing this about me.

So this is as far as we get.

I couldn't continue exposing Asuna, our friends, and even Yui to this horrible agony any longer.

With fingers that had barely any feeling, I somehow managed to grab the hilt of my sword, and I tried to lift it.

At that very moment, I heard a splash on the right, followed by light, quick footsteps. Mutasina's head turned. Despite the stiffness, I managed to turn to my right.

Running through the water, splashing mightily, with long black hair and a white dress...was Yui.

She rushed straight at Mutasina with a determined look in her eyes. Her sword wasn't drawn, but there was red light in her hands, and the Noose glowed blue around her tiny neck.

Yui was an AI, but she could receive sensory information through her avatar. That included heat, cold, and pain, which she interpreted as pleasant or unpleasant, like a human would. That was one of the core aspects of Akihiko Kayaba's AI design, and even Yui herself said that she expected not being able to breathe would immobilize her with the same agony that we felt. So how...?

When Mutasina saw her, she leaped backward and tucked the staff under her arm, starting a dark magic by hand. But her motion was awkward since she was holding the staff with her arm against her side.

Noticing this, Yui made an arrow-pulling motion with her reddened hands. Her left hand extended, and with the right pulled back to her shoulder, a narrow line of flames appeared. It was the starter Fire Magic skill technique, Flame Arrow.

Yui aimed it as she ran and clenched her hands without hesitation.

Shwa! The arrow flew forward. Mutasina grabbed her staff again and knocked it away. The arrow burst into sparks and dispersed. That was a similar trick to my spell-blasting technique—but it forced her to cancel the dark magic gesture, and she didn't have time to start over.

Now just ten feet away, Yui drew her short sword from her left side and jumped mightily.

"Yaaaaah!" she roared, fierce despite her youth. Her small body arched as far as it could in the air, unleashing a vicious strike.

Mutasina, meanwhile, lifted the staff with both hands to block Yui's sword.

Claaaang! It caused a metallic clash, throwing out white sparks that lit the countenances of the combatants.

The glowing bluish-purple gem in the tip of Mutasina's staff flickered for just a moment. And at that moment, I felt the sticky object stuck in my throat quiver. So it was true…The effect of the Noose was connected to that staff.

Yui bounced backward and resumed her attack as soon as she landed again. This time, she did not attempt a large swing, but a blindingly fast sequence of swipes. However, Mutasina accurately blocked each one with her staff.

I couldn't help but be stunned—when had Yui's skill with the blade gotten so good? She must have been practicing for all she was worth with Alice while we were away at school. I sensed a kind of kindred style with the knight in her movements.

But sadly, her moves were too honest.

That wasn't a bad thing, in and of itself. If anything, it was a shortcut to improvement. She could learn tricks like feints and sleight of hand later.

But the reason that Alice's precise and bold style worked was because of the tremendous speed and weight behind it. Yui's style had plenty of speed, but not much weight. And that meant that even a mage like Mutasina could easily deflect her attacks.

She made to block Yui's high slice—but it was a feint, and she stepped out of the way to avoid it. Yui's sword hit nothing but air, and she lost her balance. Mutasina responded with a left knee. The plated long boots she wore went up over the knee, and that hard surface smashed Yui's little body away as she lunged forward.

My rage at Mutasina and my own impotence reached its peak, and my vision doubled again.

Nearby, Asuna was growling somehow, despite her blocked windpipe, and trying to get up. But she stumbled and fell to the ground again. The suffocation was overriding all of her senses, preventing her avatar from moving.

Yui fell onto the rocks on her back and yelped, "Augh!" That single blow took out nearly 20 percent off her HP. But it only stopped her for a second; she rose quickly, brushing the sand off her cheek and readying her sword again.

Mutasina, who'd been handling her without expression, let her mouth curl with displeasure. She moved the staff to one hand and stuck her free hand into her robe to extract a thin dagger. The blade was as sharp as a clock hand and gleamed coldly in the light exuding from the staff head.

Mutasina was going to kill her.

I struggled against the burning pain in my lungs, trying to think. I couldn't stand with willpower alone. I had to do something to put the suffocating feeling at bay, if just for a few seconds. Could I overwrite it with something stronger, like pain? No, the pain setting in this game wasn't as bad as in the Underworld, and I couldn't hold my sword anyway. I could move my hands, but at best, I could only curl my fingers...

A single idea popped into my head, crackling with electricity.

There were no guarantees it would work. If I failed, I would probably be cut off by the AmuSphere's safety measures. But I had to try it.

Awkwardly spreading my fingers, I formed a circle with my hands, touching the fingertips together: the gesture for decay magic. That was just enough to be recognized as a successful motion, as a green-gray light spread over my hands.

Out of the corner of my eye, I saw Yui readying her short sword, while Mutasina responded by flipping her dagger over into a backhand grip.

Not yet. Mutasina hadn't noticed my plan yet. Right in front of me, Dia had her eyes clamped shut as she withstood the agony, so she hadn't noticed the color of my magic. Using her body as a visual shield, I judged the proper timing.

Yui's little form was bent fully forward, her sword held back on the right side. That was the motion for Rage Spike, a low charging skill. Light blue covered her blade, and the air was full of a high-pitched thrum...

Now!

I opened my mouth as wide as I could and pointed my hands at it. At point-blank range, I didn't need to aim. I clenched my hands, and the gray sphere held in them—the Decay Magic starter spell, Rotten Shot—flew into my mouth with a horrifying squelch.

First, my nose stung with a truly indescribable stench, far worse than any and every smell I'd experienced in my life to that point. Next, a flavor like boiled despair spread throughout my mouth. Tears welled up in my eyes, and my stomach roiled. An overwhelming urge to vomit rose from my gut, tearing open the blockage I felt deep in my throat. It didn't mean I could breathe again, but at least the paralysis was gone.

I could move.

"Aaaaaaaaah!!"

I turned my urge to hurl into a roar, squeezing my sword and leaping up from my prone position. In an instant, I had leaped over Dia and rushed toward Mutasina. The witch glanced my way, and her eyes bolted open with shock. On pure reflexes, she lifted the staff with her right hand.

Gray light spilled through my gritted teeth as I wound up my sword in the air. The instant my body went into the Vertical posture, the sword itself told me, "You can go farther." I deepened the stance, and the sword's vibration strengthened.

"Yaaaah!!" I roared again, activating the four-part Vertical

Square, whose proficiency requirements I suspected had only just recently been unlocked.

Mutasina's long staff blocked the first strike from above, producing an ear-wrenching sound. The blade sank nearly half an inch into the staff's head, and although the gem flickered violently, it was not enough to sever it. If I'd only used Vertical, I'd probably have taken a dagger counterattack to my side, too.

The second and third attacks were thrusting slashes, high and low. Mutasina rotated her staff and blocked them both. Based on the speed of her reaction, she was familiar with Vertical Square. Undeterred, I placed all my strength into the fourth and final swing downward.

Mutasina dropped her dagger and used both hands to hold the staff up sideways.

The blue light of my sword skill reflected in her dark, wide-open eyes.

I swung the sword not toward the staff, but at the spot between those eyes.

This one did not have the same powerful shock to it. Instead, there was a pleasing *crack!* and the sword's path continued down close to the ground, where the rest of its force dissipated into a circle of rising dust.

All was silent for a moment.

Mutasina's right and left hands held the long staff—but they were now separated by space.

Black flames spurted from the sliced ends of each half of the staff and quickly spread to the entire weapon. The blue-purple gem crumbled quietly, and the shards burned away in the air.

Next, a red damage effect glowed on Mutasina's forehead. She tossed the burning staff aside, pressed her left hand to the space between her eyes, and took a stumbling step backward.

There was also heatless flames burning on my neck as I waited for the post-skill paralysis to wane. The instant I could feel that the Noose was burning away, the blockage in my throat simply vanished.

"Ahhh..."

I expelled all the air from my lungs, then greedily sucked in a breath of cold, fresh air. The aftertaste of the Rotten Shot still lingered in my mouth, but the deliciousness of the air helped cover up the stench. I could have stood there, just enjoying the act of breathing for several minutes, but the battle wasn't over. Right behind me were Viola and Dia, and farther back on the sandbank were Magis and the body double, who had all been freed from the Noose as well. I had to eliminate Mutasina from this world before any of them could interfere.

I squeezed the sword in my hand and rose.

The witch stared at me with her right eye, still holding her forehead. I couldn't see any traces of anger or hatred in her half-exposed features. If anything, there was a faint smile on her lips. It didn't seem like a bluff...She probably still had some come-from-behind trick up her sleeve.

Behind me, I heard the high-pitched clang of swords meeting, and a voice cried out, "Go, Kirito!"

Most likely, Asuna was holding back the recovered twins on her own. The others were fanning out along the water's edge to keep the rest of Mutasina's army at bay. I couldn't hesitate now. If Mutasina had a secret attack ready, I had to cut her down with it.

I pulled the sword back on the right and leaned forward, in the stance for the low charging skill, Rage Spike. Without her staff or dagger, Mutasina had no means of defending against it.

The witch was still smiling. I stared into her eyes, which seemed as dark as the vacuum of space, and prepared to activate the skill.

But at that very moment, thick, choking smoke billowed up from the left side, blotting out my vision. I smelled nothing and had no difficulty breathing. It wasn't smoke, specifically, but pure darkness with no physical form.

Suddenly, I felt a presence just to my left. A voice said, "You have my highest compliments for this, Kirito. I hope we meet again."

It was the voice of "Sensei" Magis, the dark mage who should have been all the way back on the sandbar. I canceled the Rage Spike and slashed out on the left side but felt nothing.

"Nobody move!" I warned my friends, waiting for the blackness to dissipate. If this was made of magic, it wouldn't last long.

As I suspected, the darkness began to fade in just ten seconds. If Magis's words weren't a ruse, he and Mutasina would have disengaged from the scene, but they couldn't have gotten far yet. Once the starlight was about half its previous brightness, I raced for the spot where Mutasina had stood.

But there was no sign of the witch or Magis. I swept my eyes from the upstream riverbed, to the woods at my west, then downstream, but I couldn't spot any human figures. It was as though they had completely vanished with the smoke.

"Kirito...," whispered a nervous voice. I turned around to see Asuna with her rapier in hand—and fortunately unhurt. Relieved, I asked, "Where are Viola and Dia...?"

"They vanished within seconds of being engulfed in that smoke. Though, they couldn't have gone far..."

"Exactly..."

Perhaps it was a double deception spell, and they were still hiding nearby. If we searched behind every rock and tree, we might find them, but there wasn't time for that—not when nearly a hundred players were facing off against Agil and Klein with weapons drawn at the water's edge.

But actually, there was one more thing.

Asuna was thinking it, too. We raced to the center of the riverbed, where Yui was standing stock-still.

"Yui!"

"Yui, honey!"

The little girl, still holding her short sword in shock, flinched and looked in our direction. An innocent smile lit up her sand-caked face.

"Papa, Mama!" Yui ran over toward us, and Asuna and I knelt down to catch and embrace her.

I still didn't know how she'd been able to move under the effect of the Noose of the Accursed, but we would have plenty of time for questions later. If Yui hadn't done her best, we would have either surrendered to Mutasina's army or been slaughtered.

How long had we been doing this?

It felt like the mood had softened, so I looked up. Over in the river, all the players in Mutasina's army had lowered their weapons and were looking at us with new expressions.

I spotted Holgar among them and got to my feet. Now that the Noose had been dispelled, they were probably realizing that they didn't need to fight anymore. But not only had they been in a wartime mood for the past three days, they'd just been swept down the river by our trap, so they might not be able to change their minds in the moment. I needed to start a serious dialogue with Holgar, who held a leadership position.

After just a step or two toward the river, another thought struck my mind, and I looked downstream at the sandbar.

But the body double I'd knocked over there was already gone.

8

I held out a hesitant chunk of raw Life Harvester meat, and a huge beak snatched it away with frightening speed, gobbling it down whole.

On my left, Kuro growled unhappily, so I gave the panther a chunk of meat, too. Then the bird of prey that owned the deadly beak chirped, prompting me to present it with another.

The bird, which was about the size of Kuro, was known as a leaden long-tailed eagle. In keeping with its name, the bird's feathers were dark gray, and the edges of its tail feathers were nearly long enough to drag on the ground. Its beak and claws were even darker than the feathers, almost entirely black except for a bluish tint to the sharp tips.

By the time we finished our negotiations with Holgar and his men, the abandoned bird's HP was nearly gone. Even still, it attempted to fulfill its heartless owner's orders and attacked us as we approached. I thought it would be a mercy to put the thing out of its misery, but Yui insisted that she wanted to save the bird.

She was the MVP of the night, after all, and I couldn't refuse a request from her. I got closer and offered some raw harve meat, expecting to get nipped. Sure enough, it attacked me with its beak without even a glance at the meat, but I kept thrusting the meat in its face as I evaded its attacks, and eventually the bird—or more accurately, the game system—gave up and allowed the taming meter to appear.

Fortunately, I had tons of harve meat on hand, so I kept feeding the beast and filling its meter bit by bit, finally succeeding after twenty long minutes. All my companions stopped to watch this process, as did the eighty-plus former members of Mutasina's army. When I finally pumped a fist in triumph, I was treated to a huge round of applause from the crowd.

Of course, I wasn't in any mood to hop right onto the bird's back, so I joined the others—including Friscoll, whom we freed from his silky prison—and walked back through the forest to Ruis na Ríg, where we started another feast in the open area by the stables. The former Mutasina army soldiers downed the roast harve and harve stew at an incredible rate, and we and the insects and the Bashin and the Patter were in no mood to be outeaten. I was certain we must have used up all the meat by now, but upon asking our head chef Asuna, she told me (terrifyingly) that "I think we've used up about twenty percent of it as of tonight."

Thinking about it, the Life Harvester was over sixty feet long. If a cow was about six feet long, then this creature was of a size that could fit twenty cattle in two rows. I thought I'd read somewhere that a single cow could make a thousand portions of barbecue, so the Life Harvester could feed twenty thousand. By that standard, consuming 20 percent of it in two feasts was actually a considerable feat.

We drank up all the beer the *Insectsite* players had brought us the last time, so Klein complained "If only we had some beer" no less than ten times, but the feast was quite lively even without the benefit of virtual alcohol. Holgar, Dikkos, and Tsuburo all but admitted that they were going to play *Unital Ring* under the threat of the Noose until they beat the game or died, so it must have been hard to describe their feeling of liberation. I felt the same way, of course.

My only concern was that we'd let the entire Virtual Study Society get away, not just Mutasina. We'd destroyed the staff, so that horrible suffocation spell was no longer possible for her to cast, I assumed, but there was no way they'd give up on their aims for *Unital Ring*. I had a feeling we'd run into them again, with another unexpected trick up their sleeve.

But that was a matter for another time. And I wouldn't allow them to torment Yui, Asuna, and my friends again.

I was sitting off to the side of the dwindling party, swearing oaths to myself as I fed my two pets dinner, when faint footsteps approached. There could only be one person who practiced such stealthy footwork as a matter of course...

"Good job today, Sinon," I said, turning to see the gunner, wearing a dark-green cloak to hide her revealing battle armor.

She blinked at being detected and replied, "Same to you. I had Holgar split up his men among the buildings in the south area."

"Did we have enough rooms...er, beds?"

"Not quite, so Liz made more on the spot. We've got plenty of materials, after all."

"I don't know if I'd be excited to sleep in a crude wood and dried-grass bed, though..."

"It's only in order to log out. They could sleep on the floor just as fine," she snapped, making me chuckle.

I decided to bring up something I hadn't been able to say at the feast. "By the way, Sinon, thanks a ton for your help. If you hadn't sniped with your musket, I wouldn't have been able to knock Mutasina to the ground," I said, bowing in thanks.

Sinon seemed conflicted about this compliment. She looked at the leaden long-tailed eagle. "The truth is: I was aiming for Mutasina, not the bird, but that was the best I could do with the musket. I was useless in the battle after that. Got to raise my accuracy a bit more..."

"Hmmm...What are the other former *GGO* players fighting with, once the grace period is over?"

"From what I've seen online, almost everyone is using crossbows or matchlocks they've found around the starting ruins."

"Matchlocks...? What are those again?"

Fortunately, Miss Sinon had an entire lecture for me. "They're guns with fuses, basically. Technically, they're classified as muskets like my gun, but mine is a flintlock musket, not a matchlock musket. Both are significantly easier to shoot than their actual counterparts in the real world, but even still, a matchlock requires you to light a fuse, so it takes a few extra seconds than a flintlock."

"Ohhh, a fuse...That seems like it'd be stressful, if you're used to all the laser rifles in *GGO*..."

"Yeah, it's a lot easier being able to fire fifty or a hundred shots in a row with a single power pack." Sinon smirked. "But once you get used to working a matchlock, it's only two or three seconds' difference from casting Flame Arrow. When you're dealing with dozens of them at once, they're a major threat...The *GGO* starting point is just to the left of *ALO*'s, so it's quite possible we'll run into them as we proceed toward the center of the world map."

"Good point...We'll need to work on developing shields and armor that can stop a bullet before then. But preferably, we can make peace with them, like with Holgar's people."

"True," Sinon admitted, looking to the night sky to the north-northeast—the direction of the land revealed by the heavenly light. "But even if we're able to cooperate with them, as we get closer to the goal, eventually we'll..."

She didn't finish the sentence, but I didn't need to hear it to know what she meant. If only one team—or one single player—could beat the game, they would eventually need to determine a winner among those who were working together. Either by dialogue, drawing straws, playing rock-paper-scissors, or as Mutasina said, by deadly combat.

"...I'm sure we'll figure out the right answer when that time comes," I told her, giving the leaden long-tailed eagle the last of the meat. The bird gobbled it down happily, then chirped "Pwee!" and started walking toward the stable behind us without needing an order. Kuro followed it, equally sated.

"...What are you going to call the bird?"

"Huh? Hmmm..."

I called the lapispine dark panther Kuro for its black color, so if I was to choose a Japanese name using the same logic, I would have to call the gray bird Haiiro, but people like Leafa would probably make fun of me for coming up with generic names again.

"So…what are some other names for the color gray?" I asked Sinon.

The bookworm lived up to her reputation, as she wasted no time in listing them off. "Well, there's *nezumiiro*, that's like mouse gray; there's *usuzumiiro*, that's the color of faint, watery ink; then there's *namariiro*, the color of lead."

"Nezumi, Usuzumi…Oh, I think I like Namari. And it's already taken a shot from your lead bullet, too."

"Not that I was aiming for it, like I said," she snapped, punching my shoulder.

I apologized, chuckling, and called after the retreating bird of prey, "Hey! Your name is Namari now, just so you know!"

The eagle's head spun around, and as if to say "It's a stupid name, but I guess I'll take it," squawked, "Pwee!"

The next day, October 2nd, Ruis na Ríg began to grow at a speed that far surpassed my initial expectations.

First, a paneled road ten feet wide was built along the east bank of the Maruba River, meaning that the unstable, rocky trip to the Stiss Ruins was suddenly remarkably easier.

The south quadrant of Ruis na Ríg now opened for business in earnest, and both surprisingly and luckily, the *Insectsite* players and Holgar's team agreed to take over managing the inn and general store and so on, meaning we no longer needed to travel to the Stiss Ruins to hire NPCs to work for us—assuming that was even possible.

Of course, the south area was also home to Lisbeth's armory, where she put out her personally crafted weapons and armor, but because iron ore was still precious, the Fine Iron series had to be sold at a premium. Asuna, Alice, and Leafa were using weapons a rank above that, in the Steel tier, but the Premium Steel Ingots that made them came from melting down my inherited weapon, the mighty Blárkveld, and we couldn't make more for the time being.

While Lisbeth was strongly pushing for a stable source of more iron ore, the most lucrative mining spot we'd discovered so far was the secret cave behind the falls down the Maruba River. We knew from testing that it was possible to craft within the cave, so I wanted to create a workspace capable of smelting ingots in there, but everything required serious labor. And we couldn't simply spend all our time focusing on running the town. Ruis na Ríg was nothing more than the beachhead we needed to journey to the center of the world.

Yes, now that five days had passed since the start of this new phase, September 27th, we had finally concluded the preparations we needed to head from our log cabin's landing point to the northeast: the land revealed by the heavenly light. We were presumably the furthest along of any *ALO* players, but there was no way to know how close any of the other games' players were to the goal. For now, all we could do was proceed with the equipment and stats we had—but before that, there was one thing I needed to know.

The next day, Saturday, October 3rd, I woke up early to leave my home in Kawagoe at five o'clock and arrived at Rath's Roppongi office in Minato Ward before the clock struck seven.

9

"Good morning, Kirigaya," said Dr. Rinko Koujiro at the security gate on the fifth floor of the building. She seemed sleepy.

"Good morning. I'm sorry to force you into the office so early in the morning," I apologized.

"It's all right. I live very close by."

"Really? Where do you live, Rinko?" I asked. Roppongi was presumably a very expensive place to live, I figured.

But Dr. Koujiro just pointed at the ceiling farther down the hall. "Two floors up."

"Ah, I see…Practically living at the office, then."

"There are two more empty apartments, so if you get hired by Rath in the future, you could live here, too."

"Ah…wait, what?!"

I panicked, because I was sure I hadn't told her that I was hoping to work for Rath in the future after school. But the professor just gave me a mysterious smile and headed down the hallway without another word.

The familiar Soul Translator room was empty.

This round of Underworld investigation would include Asuna and Alice, but my scheduled arrival was two hours earlier than theirs. That was because we had logged out in very different places at the end of the previous session, which meant I needed to travel inside the simulation to the coordinates where they would log in. Barring any trouble, the travel itself wouldn't take more than half an hour, but after the series of unexpected situations last time, I couldn't take anything for granted. I would need to walk as quietly and surreptitiously as possible down the streets back to the Arabel mansion.

With this mission at the forefront of my mind, I took off my jacket and went to lie down on one of the two STLs. Dr. Koujiro input some commands on the tablet controller so the gel bed automatically adjusted its density to fit my body better.

"As I've said many times before," she started to say, but I cut her off.

"Safety is the top priority, I know. If anything happens, I'll log out right away."

I lifted my left hand and folded in my fingers in a staggered order: pinkie, middle, thumb, ring, index. It was an awkward demonstration, which earned me a smirk from the professor.

"I'm serious, though," she said. "If anything happens to you again, I won't have any excuse to give your parents this time."

"I'll keep it at the forefront of my mind at every moment. And my parents aside, I'm sure that Asuna's dad would sue you for any trouble…"

"If the former CEO of RCT took us to court, I'm sure that even Lieutenant Colonel Kikuoka would have trouble wriggling out of that one."

"…Speaking of which, what's his public position now? I met him enjoying some fine cakes in Ginza, but I thought that, on paper, Ground Self-Defense Force's Lieutenant Colonel Seijirou Kikuoka *died* on the *Ocean Turtle*," I pointed out.

For some reason, Dr. Koujiro made an annoyed face and shrugged. "Unfortunately, I can't tell you that. He said he would show up around this evening, so if you see him, you can ask him for yourself. Are you all set?"

I pushed the mental image of Kikuoka's smirk out of my head and nodded. "Yes, good to go."

"Then let's get started. Just remember, once you've finished traveling to your end point, log out immediately. Got that?"

"Understood."

She made a face that said she didn't believe me, but she tapped on the tablet screen anyway. The STL's overhead block slid down and covered my head.

A mysterious sound like the lapping of waves filled my consciousness, separating my fluctlight from waking reality and transporting me to a far-off land.

As the tunnel of blinding light whisked me through, I tried to recall the situation when I had last logged out. I couldn't have forgotten it...I was sitting in the back seat of the black luxury vehicle with the circled-cross logo and about to shake hands with a mystery man who called himself the Integrity Pilot commander, when a disconnect command from the real world forcibly extracted me from the simulation.

......Wait a second.

I hadn't considered this before. Could that mean I would reappear...?

"Aaaah?!" I shrieked the moment my eyelids opened.

That was because a huge truck was racing right for me. I nearly created an Incarnate wall in front of me, only stopping myself just in time. Doing so would have crushed the truck and caused a reading on those Incarnameters, sending those friendly police officers—er, the North Centoria Imperial Guard—to pay me a visit.

Instead, I was going to leap to the right out of the way, but it wasn't actually necessary.

With the blast of a whistle, the truck slowed down. I could see a man in a light-gray cloak standing in front of the truck, holding a glowing red baton sideways in a command to stop.

The truck came to a halt, put its right-turn indicator on, then eventually moved lanes and ran just to the left of me. Breathing a sigh of relief, I felt I finally had the leeway to examine where I was in wider detail.

I was standing in the center lane of a three-lane road. The sky was clear, but the angle of the sunlight was shallow. The Underworld time of day was synchronized with the real clock, so it was also just after seven in the morning here. Many automobiles— wait, was it mechamobiles?—drove through the lanes on either side. Any car in the middle lane was stopped by the man in the gray cloak and forced to change lanes.

I had logged out of the last session in the middle of a car ride. So naturally, the next time I went back in, I appeared at the same coordinates—I just didn't consider that *other cars* might be traveling in that same space. But it seemed that someone in this world had anticipated that possibility and placed a traffic management specialist here for me.

In fact, the spot where I was standing was surrounded by yellow-painted poles and chains. I logged out on this spot around 5:10 PM on September 30th, so that meant they had placed this traffic impediment here for over sixty hours in the middle of a major traffic artery, just for the sake of a man whose return time was a total unknown.

I walked over to the man in the gray coat, whose back was to me, and spoke up to express my appreciation for his efforts.

"Um, thank you…"

He bolted around with alarm and stared at me for several seconds, as if looking at a ghost. At last, he stammered, "Y…y-y-you…you're real…"

"Um, y-yes?"

"S-sorry, nothing. I'm from the North Centoria Traffic Bureau. You must be Kirito, right?" said the man, who was in his thirties and looked quite earnest.

"That's right," I said.

"Then please get in that mechamobile over there," he said, pointing off to the left. Between the first lane and the spacious sidewalk, there was a parking lane of the sort seen in Europe and North America, where a beautiful deep-blue midsize sedan was waiting. I didn't see any writing on the side, but the silver circled-cross insignia shone on the front door.

"B-but I need to go somewhere…"

"A car from the city guard will come shortly, and that will only make matters more complicated. Move quickly!"

His tone was so urgent that I couldn't argue any further. This man had been braving the chill of midwinter—taken in shifts, I assumed—to manage traffic on my account, after all.

"…All right, I will. Um, thank you so much," I said, bowing deeply. The man's eyes widened, and he gave me a crisp salute. Next, he used his traffic baton to stop the number one lane, and I stepped over the chains and ran for the blue car on the side of the road. The left rear door opened as I rushed around the back, and a quiet voice said, "Please, get in."

At this point, I couldn't argue much. Asuna and Alice were scheduled to dive in at nine o'clock, so I just had to make sure I was at the Arabel mansion by then.

Discarding my hesitation, I slid into the rear seat of the car, and the door shut automatically behind me. Only the driver was inside, so it must have been operable from the front seat, like a real-world taxi.

The moment I was in my seat, the mechamobile put its right blinker on and smoothly rolled into motion. The fact that it would react to the heat element just from stepping on the accelerator, without needing to run an engine, made it more like an electric vehicle. I had assumed that the level of scientific tech in the Underworld was around the post-WWII era of the real world. But aside from the lack of computers, everything else seemed to be slightly more advanced than that, actually.

Exhaling, I took a look at the driver, who had been totally silent since that first request. The driver wore a dark-blue uniform nearly the same color as the car, which matched the uniform worn by Stica Schtrinen and Laurannei Arabel when they rescued me from the interrogation room at the city guard's office. But this driver was neither of them. Based on his voice, I suspected he was a young man.

It was at this moment that the driver spoke up again. "Pardon me. I'm Operator Second Class Lagi Quint of the Underworld Space Force, Integrity Pilothood. I was ordered to escort you to the space force base."

"H-hi, I'm Kirito."

I felt disappointed that I had no official title to attach to my name, but "Second Year Student, Returnee School" didn't sound very impressive, and I would die of embarrassment if I introduced myself as the Black Swordsman. To be strictly accurate, Alice arrested me when I was the sixth-rank elite disciple at North Centoria Imperial Swordcraft Academy, so I hadn't graduated yet, but it was two hundred years ago, so all the records would have been purged by now.

It wasn't clear where in the Pilothood's hierarchy "operator second class" rested, but based on the firm look in Lagi's eyes, he didn't seem to be the type open to small talk. I looked out the window instead at the scenery running past, including mechamobiles large and small.

After ten seconds, I finally noticed something. "Wait…You said we were going to the base? Isn't your base outside of Centoria…?" I asked, leaning forward.

"That's right," said Lagi, keeping his eyes on the road. "There's a bit of traffic, so it will take about thirty minutes to get there."

"Um…I need to be at the Arabel mansion by nine o'clock…"

The analog clock embedded in the mechamobile's dashboard said it was 7:28. If we got to the base by eight, I doubted they would let me go in another thirty minutes, after the trouble they'd gone through to control traffic for me, and there was no guarantee they'd give me a ride to the Arabel house.

But Operator Second Class Lagi simply said, "I'm aware of that. Your companions will be greeted by someone else."

"Oh…uh, th-thanks…"

I bowed again, but even still, I needed to tell Asuna and Alice about this before they dived in, which required logging out. How did the Integrity Pilots process the way that I just appeared and disappeared without a trace?

In any case, if truly necessary, I could escape from any place. And though I didn't want to do it, I could break through walls with Incarnation or cut through them with a sword...

That was when I belatedly realized I was unarmed.

Of course. Before I got arrested by the guards in our previous dive, I'd handed the Night-Sky Blade and Blue Rose Sword to Asuna and Alice. They would be able to return the swords when we met up again, but I would have no weapons until then. If only we had an inventory system in this world, I'd be able to pull out a sword or two or three or four, but sadly, it was not that convenient here.

If they can give us a status window, they could at least give us a usable inventory, I grumbled to Chief Researcher Takeru Higa in the real world, before leaning back against the seat again.

The mechamobile headed north up the core road that split the center of North Centoria, passing the city center (which seemed bigger than I remembered) before proceeding through a grand gate out of the city.

With one less lane now, the road continued north. Spacious farm fields and pastures stretched out on either side, bounded by mammoth white walls that glowed with the morning sun. Those were the Everlasting Walls that split the human realm into four pieces, national borders that Administrator had erected centuries ago, still present so many years later.

Amid the farms on the left side was an occasional glimpse of blue running through it: the surface of the Rul River. And straight ahead, far over the horizon, loomed the curve of the End Mountains that surrounded the realm.

At their foot, I would probably still find the village of Rulid today. But none of the people I knew were there anymore. Sister Azalia, Old Man Garitta, Elder Gasfut...and of course, Eugeo.

I clasped my hands, struck by another wave of longing and homesickness.

But I had to accept it already. Not a single one of the people I loved was still alive in this world. If I got teary-eyed every time I thought about Ronie, Tiese, and Sortiliena, I wouldn't be able to fulfill my mission.

And technically speaking, there was still one person I might possibly meet again: Alice's sister, Selka Zuberg. She'd been placed in a deep freeze, to await her sister's return on the eightieth floor of Central Cathedral.

Seijirou Kikuoka's mission for me was to learn the identity and intentions of the person who'd broken into the Underworld. But before that, I wanted to bring Alice and Selka together. That possibility was the one thing that was keeping Alice going in her time in the real world.

Meanwhile, the mechamobile's left-turn indicator was on. It turned off the main road onto a gentle ramp until it faced a massive structure in the distance.

It was a trapezoid pyramid shape, supported by a complex truss system. It wasn't all that tall, I thought at first, but that was only in comparison to Central Cathedral. The pyramid had to be at least three hundred feet tall on its own.

The dull silver exterior was 80 percent metal and 20 percent glass. Even in the real world, it would look like near-future architecture.

"So that's the space force base…?" I murmured.

"That's correct," replied Lagi, his voice swelling with undisguised pride.

"And who, uh, designed it?"

"It is said that His Majesty the Star King did it himself."

There you are again, Star King!

My lips twisted into a wry grimace as I replied, "Ah, I see." Lagi glanced at me through his rear view mirror but said nothing else.

If the trapezoidal pyramid-shaped command center of the Centoria base of the Underworld Space Force was huge, it was only keeping up with the size of the grounds.

After passing through some kind of security checkpoint at an imposing front gate, the silver building was beyond a parking garage so huge that it could probably store all the mechamobiles in Centoria. I assumed we were heading for the building, of course, but the mechamobile turned left in front of the garage and moved to the south side of the base.

Eventually, I saw a large water surface ahead on the left. I called up a mental map of the area outside of North Centoria and deduced that this was probably Lake Norkia.

Thick forest ran along the western side of the lake. The car took a right turn, then a left, passed through another gate, and headed into the forest. We spent several minutes on the road, dark under the heavy tree canopy despite the morning sun, until finally reaching an ancient-looking iron gate. I didn't see any guards, but somehow, the two sides of the gate opened automatically as the mechamobile approached. A little while later down the road, the trees suddenly opened up.

In the center of the circular clearing, which measured a good hundred yards across, there sat a very old-looking mansion. The composition of the scene reminded me of our log cabin in the Great Zelletelio Forest, but this building looked completely different. The walls were gray stone, and the roof was blackish stone slate. It was three stories but with very few windows, giving it a fortress-like appearance.

But despite being winter, the flower planters in the front garden were blooming wildly, which did counteract some of the coldness of the building. If not for those flowers, I might assume they were bringing me here to kidnap or eliminate me.

The mechamobile trundled over the worn cobblestones and came to a stop at last before the mansion. It was exactly eight o'clock, just as he'd told me.

The left door opened on its own, and Lagi said, "Thank you for your patience, Kirito. We're here."

"Thank *you* for the drive. And for waiting on the street all those days," I said, a bit of extra encouragement, before stepping out of the car.

The mingling scents of the forest and flowers were refreshing, and I filled my lungs. The sound of the front door of the mansion opening drew my attention.

What I saw there caused me to hold back the breath I was about to expel.

Crossing the entrance porch and descending the short set of steps was a thin man in a perfectly pressed uniform the same color as Lagi's, wearing a cylindrical hat pulled low over a white leather mask.

It was Eolyne Herlentz, commander of the Integrity Pilots.

I was so stunned that I merely stood rooted to the spot as he approached, boots clicking. When Eolyne reached me, he lifted the brim of his hat ever so slightly and said, "Forgive me for not removing my hat, Kirito. It's a rather bright and sunny day for this season."

Midwinter seemed like an odd time to complain about the sun being too strong, I thought, but then I recalled what this man had said to me in the car three days ago. Eolyne claimed that he hid the top half of his face behind the mask because the skin around his eyes was weak to the light of Solus.

"Oh…it's cool. I don't mind," I said, letting out the breath I'd been holding at last. Eolyne smiled faintly. It seemed more cynical than warm, and I suddenly realized that while I'd maintained a formal politeness with Operator Second Class Lagi Quint, I was speaking to the Integrity Pilot commander as if we were equals. Thankfully, he didn't seem to mind.

I could see Eolyne blink behind the thin glass lens in the aperture of his mask. He extended his right hand. "I'm delighted to see you like this. Hello again, Kirito."

I'd been about to shake his hand when I got logged out last time. I hesitated, imagining that it might happen again, but it wasn't so late that Dr. Koujiro was going to pull me out yet.

"…Nice to meet you," I said, summoning my determination and clasping Eolyne's thin, long fingers in my own.

No, sparks did not fly in my brain, nor did I suddenly receive a flood of new information.

His skin was just a little bit cold. His grip was strong, contrary to his delicate appearance. That was the extent of what I felt from the contact.

After just a second, he let go, his facial expression unchanging. He glanced over my shoulder and said, "Thank you for driving, Lagi. You may return to the base now; I'll contact Captain Feagle."

I turned to see Lagi, who was standing by the mechamobile, giving Eolyne a swift salute before he rotated to my direction and faced forward again. "Understood, Commander. Operator Second Class Quint, returning to Cattleya Company."

He lowered his hand and got back into the vehicle, then smoothly turned it around and traveled back the way we'd come. As I watched the taillights recede, I thought, *Now how am I going to get back to Centoria?* I'd just have to trust Lagi that Asuna and Alice would be given a ride of their own.

"Come this way," Eolyne said, beckoning me up the steps leading to the mansion's door.

He brought me to what appeared to be a tearoom on the east end of the second floor. The hallway was dark enough that lights were needed even during the day, but in here, the morning sun got through the lattice windows on the south and east wall well enough. For a "tearoom," it was still larger than the combined living and dining room at the Kirigaya household, with furniture as deluxe as anything at Central Cathedral. But everything, including the building itself, was so old-fashioned and worn that you could call them antiques. It stood out even more, being attached to the futuristic space force base.

Despite the many questions I was burning to ask, Commander Eolyne sat me down on the sofa by the window, then disappeared into the adjacent room. Eventually, a fragrant smell came drifting over, which did quite a number on my still-empty stomach.

But whether I ate in the real world or not, it would have no effect on my sense of hunger in the Underworld. That meant that before my fluctlight had descended into this body, it had already been several hours since its last meal. I hadn't eaten anything with young Phercy at the Arabel mansion, and the city guards who took me in for questioning didn't even offer a steaming bowl of pork cutlet and rice to tempt me into talking. On my first dive into space following the maximum acceleration phase, Stica and Laurannei escorted us to the Arabel house, where they served some light sandwiches...Was that the last meal I'd had here?

This cascading realization upgraded my hunger into starvation, and I started to wonder if I would get in trouble for using Incarnation to transform one of the knickknacks on the table into a donut when Eolyne returned at last.

He had removed his coat and hat. My eyes were drawn to the flaxen hair that hung over his mask, so it wasn't until a few moments later that I noticed he was carrying a large tray containing cups, a pot, a water jug, and other odds and ends. I was so startled by the commander himself preparing the tea that I rose from the couch in a half stance, where he stopped me.

"You may remain seated."

I did as he said. Eolyne crossed the carpeted floor with practiced ease until he reached the sofas and set down the tray on the low table. He removed a cup and saucer and set them down in front of me, then poured the liquid from the pot. The scent was similar to coffee but not quite the same: the familiar delight of cofil tea.

Eolyne filled his own cup next, then put the pot back on the tray and set out a plate that was probably the source of the smell that had been amplifying my hunger for the past few minutes. It held a pair of round golden pastries, about four inches in diameter. Could they be?

"Are those honey pies from the Jumping Deer?" I asked.

Eolyne paused in what he was doing, then replied, "Yes. I'm surprised you're familiar with it."

"I ate them many times, long ago. The name popped up in the car the other day, too."

"Unfortunately, I bought these last week and kept them frozen until today."

"Frozen? But they're so hot…," I murmured with surprise. On the one-seat sofa to the right of the table, Eolyne's masked face curled into a smirk.

"You have ovens in the real world, don't you?"

"Um, yes. Good point…"

"It's not as good as buying them fresh from the bakery, of course, but I've put lots of research into how to reheat them. Go on, eat up."

He motioned to me, and I didn't need any further encouragement. I thanked him, then first took a sip from the steaming cup. I was so distracted by the thought of the pies that I didn't think to let my cofil tea cool first, and I gulped the boiling-hot liquid down.

"Aaaah!" I yelped, earning me a very slightly annoyed look from Eolyne, then a glass full of ice water from the pitcher. I quickly cooled my throat with a nice long drink, then thanked him and reached for a honey pie this time. He had placed little forks next to the plate, but poking at the pies was against the point. I grabbed one, opened wide, and took a big bite.

The crispy texture of the pie crust, the rich sweetness of the honey baked into the filling, the refreshing scent of siral…Nothing about the pie had changed in two hundred years. I felt as though the crust texture was slightly lighter when I bought and ate them at the Jumping Deer's storefront, but it was a minor difference.

I had eaten half the piece in a trance before I finally sighed and murmured, "It's good."

Instantly, I felt several emotions I'd been holding back bubble up all at once, and I shivered involuntarily.

The room had a traditional Norlangarth interior design. I was surrounded by the scent of cofil and flavor of honey pie. On top of that, Commander Eolyne's gentle voice and the winter morning sun shining off his flaxen hair. All these things combined to pry with compelling force at the lid I kept over my memories.

I wanted to stand up, reach over to grab Eolyne's shoulders, and shout, "Take off that mask and show me your face! What's your connection to Eugeo anyway?"

But something the Integrity Pilot commander wore about him just barely kept me seated on the couch.

It was like a barrier: invisible, extremely thin, but unbelievably strong. There was an impenetrable wall around his heart that prevented me from getting any closer, something I'd never felt from Eugeo.

Wringing out all the Incarnation I had, I placed the half-eaten honey pie on the plate and took another sip of cofil tea. The mixture of bitterness and acidity was just the way I...no, Eugeo liked it.

"It's good," I repeated, drawing a chuckle from Eolyne, who had grabbed a pie from the plate just the way I did.

"Shouldn't the legendary Star King have a better vocabulary than that?"

"...I keep telling you, I'm nothing as fancy as that." I shrugged. "I've told Stica and Laurannei many times that I have no memory at all following the Otherworld War. I don't even remember where I lived in that time."

"In other words, you have no evidence to deny this claim?" Eolyne pointed out.

Oh yeah, I realized, then shook my head. "B-but the Star King ruled over two planets at once, right? That's not my style at all. Plus, the names of the Star King and Queen were stricken from all the records, from what I hear. Why did Stica and Laurannei and you think I was the Star King? Um...sir," I added hastily. "Also..."

Eolyne held up a hand to stop me in my tracks. "Not so fast. I can't answer any of your questions if you keep asking them."

"Oh...sorry."

I finished the other half of my cup of cofil tea to calm myself down. Eolyne promptly poured me more, so this time I added a little bit of cream. The sight of the marbling effect as it swirled on the surface struck me as strange.

"...That's not milk in this tiny pot, it's cream. Did the Underworld have cream before...?"

"It is said that the King and Queen discovered the process to make it."

"...Oh. Uh-huh."

"And you can just call me Eolyne; you don't have to say *sir* or *commander*. I'd prefer to just call you Kirito anyway."

"Er, sorry, I just..."

I lost my composure a bit, thinking it was an indirect bit of sarcasm, but the commander's mouth maintained the same subtle smile as before. While I considered what to say, Eolyne added some cream to his own cofil and gently stirred it in with a silver spoon.

"I almost never have the chance to have someone call me that anyway. I consider it a valuable experience."

"W-well, if you insist, I can do that...By the way, is the Herlentz family a really famous name?"

The cup paused on its way to his lips. But it was not out of outrage or displeasure; he stared at me for a moment, then chuckled softly. "I see. If your memory only lasts until two hundred years ago, I guess it only makes sense that you wouldn't know. Well...in a sense, it is famous. The Herlentz family was founded by the legendary hero and first Integrity Knight commander, who fought the dark god Vecta in the Otherworld War: Bercouli Herlentz."

"...?!"

I was so shocked that I nearly spit out the cofil tea with cream onto Eolyne's face. Thankfully, I swallowed it instead and exhaled with relief that I didn't choke. Carefully returning the cup to its saucer, I made my surprise known in a different, safer way.

"Th-that was that old guy...er, Commander Bercouli's last name?!"

Eolyne suddenly fell silent, still holding his cup. Then he shook his head and murmured, "So…you really *have* met Bercouli the Hero. I'm actually starting to feel like you indeed came here two centuries ago."

I had to hold my tongue to keep from adding that it was only two months ago for me. I still wasn't sure yet exactly how well Eolyne and the girls understood the connection between the Underworld and the real world.

Instead, after another bite of the honey pie, I said, "Well…I really only exchanged a few words with him, at best. My partner traded blows with him in a one-on-one duel, but I was somewhere else at the time."

"Partner?" asked Eolyne curiously. I opened my mouth.

His name was Eugeo. He had the same voice, the same hair, and probably the same color eyes as you.

But with difficulty, I swallowed those words. If I mentioned Eugeo's name, Eolyne might react in some way. And the thought of what might happen if he did *nothing* sapped the courage to attempt this test.

"…Yes. He did so much to help me…More of a best friend than a partner…," I answered haltingly, before getting back to the matter at hand. "More importantly, the knight commander I knew was named Bercouli Synthesis One…And I'm pretty sure the Integrity Knights didn't have families…"

"Hmm. How should I explain…?"

Eolyne sank into the luxurious sofa seat and crossed his leg over the other. He folded his hands over his knee and waved the polished toe of his boot back and forth.

"Before becoming an Integrity Knight, Bercouli was an adventurer who traveled from the capital to the northernmost reaches of Norlangarth. Did you know that?" he asked casually.

I was about to say that I did, but I stopped myself.

Until two centuries ago, everyone believed the *story* that the Integrity Knights were protectors of the Axiom Church, summoned from the heavens—even the knights themselves. Either the truth was widely known in this era or Eolyne knew this fact because it was part of his privilege as commander of the Pilothood. I wasn't sure which, but I decided to match his story.

"Y-yeah...my partner told me about that. It's treated like a children's fairy tale, isn't it?"

"That's right. You can buy many children's storybooks about Bercouli in bookshops across Centoria. Although most of the stories were created posthumously...At any rate, before he left Centoria, Bercouli belonged to the Herlentz family."

"...I see. So that's his story..."

The Integrity Knight named Eldrie Synthesis Thirty-One had originally been Eldrie Woolsburg, I knew. So it would make sense that the other knights had their own family names—assuming they weren't peasants from the rural countryside, where people didn't always have them.

"But was there always a noble family in North Centoria called the Herlentzes...?"

Nearly all the children of noble families attended the Imperial Swordcraft Academy, so I heard many famous names while I was there, but Herlentz was completely unfamiliar to me.

Eolyne just shrugged. "It would make sense that you didn't know about it. The Herlentz family had no heir around the year 100 HE, and the line died out. The name was revived with the child Bercouli had with the knight's second commander, Fanatio Synthesis Two. Their child became the third commander of the knighthood and called himself Berche Herlentz Forty."

"Gahk!" I coughed, nearly spitting up my cofil tea.

"Kirito, are you all right?" he asked, getting up. But I held out a hand to stop him as I collected my breath.

"F...Fanatio and Bercouli had a kid?! They were...like that?!"

"They were, but...how did you not know that?"

"I just...Well, the Fanatio I knew was the kind of career-driven woman who would kill any man who looked upon her bare face, so...," I mumbled.

But then I remembered meeting Fanatio again at the Eastern Gate after the war—and how different she had seemed. She wasn't covering her face with her helmet anymore, and she was a helpful and reliable elder-sister type who was very kind to Asuna and me.

If this was true, however, it would mean that she was already carrying Bercouli's child at the time. The baby was born just a few months after peace was made with the Dark Territory. It was tearing me up inside that I didn't have any memories of that point.

The truth was, in fact, that completing my current mission in the Underworld *required* memory of what happened after the Otherworld War. Was there any way to regain at least fifty years of memories, if not all two hundred? But then my mental age would be seventy. Would that completely change my personality...?

I shook my head to clear these thoughts and stared at Eolyne. Though half his face was hidden, everything else about him reminded me exactly of Eugeo, from his build to his little gestures. From the time I first encountered him in the last dive until today, I'd entertained the thought that maybe he was some descendant of Eugeo's.

If his story was true, however, Eolyne was not a descendant of Eugeo, but of Bercouli.

"Hmmmm...," I grumbled. I could sense that, behind his mask, the pilot commander's brows were knit, so I hastened to explain, "It's just—I don't mean to be rude, but you know, you don't look very much like Bercouli..."

A cynical smile curved at the edges of Eolyne's mouth, the one way in which he did not resemble Eugeo.

"That would make sense. I was adopted into the Herlentz family."

"A...adopted? Meaning...you have no blood relation to Bercouli...?"

"I very much doubt it. The present chairman of the Stellar

Unification Council, Orvas Herlentz, still bears a passing resemblance to Bercouli's portrait."

"Orvas..."

I repeated this new name several times in my head. That was definitely a new one to me.

"So does that mean...this Orvas is your father?"

"That's right. My adoptive father, strictly speaking."

I could sense just a bit of stiffness in Eolyne's speech, and I found myself staring straight into his eyes through the holes of the leather mask.

"...What is it?"

"Oh, er...I was just wondering if maybe you and your father weren't on the best terms..."

The pilot commander's mouth dropped open. Then he smirked deeper than any I'd seen thus far—or perhaps it was just an expression of embarrassment.

"Oh, goodness...No, we're not on bad terms at all. I'm grateful to him for raising me, and I respect him as a soldier and a statesman. I believe he probably loves me just as much as if I were his true son," he said quietly, looking out the window and then suddenly back to me. "Why am I talking about this with someone I've only just met?"

"Don't worry about it. Just continue that thought."

"You are...a very strange man. Very well, I'll tell you. I've always had a good relationship with my father. But his three biological children...particularly my brother who is one year older than me is at a rather difficult age in his life."

"A difficult age...? How old are you, Eolyne?"

"Twenty."

Two years older, I thought, then realized my mistake. I was two years older in this world than in reality, which meant...

"You're my age," I murmured, staring at the spotless white mask. "Wait, so you're running the Integrity Pilothood at age twenty? But the Integrity Pilots are in charge of both the terrestrial army and the space force, aren't they? Um…I apologize if this comes off as rude, but aren't you a little young to be leading the entire military like that?"

"Yes, much too young," Eolyne replied without anger. He sighed deeply. "But the position of Integrity Pilothood commander is the only job in all public offices of the Underworld that is designated personally by the previous person to hold the title. The only qualification is that you are a member of the pilothood, with no restrictions on age or birth. Eight months ago, in April of Stellar Year 582, I was named the successor to this position by the previous commander. The person has the right to decline, and the Star King can veto, but the Star King has been gone for thirty years, and I didn't have any choice but to say no…"

"…Why not?"

"I can go into that later…The point is: My father is very pleased that I am leading the Integrity Pilothood at my age, but my brother is not pleased at all. And it has caused considerable tension between my father and my brother."

He spread his hands to demonstrate his lack of power to fix the situation. I glanced at the building looming beyond the trees and asked, "Is your brother also an Integrity Pilot?"

"No, he's in the ground force. Their base is outside of South Centoria, so there are few opportunities for the two of us to meet in person."

"I see…"

That meant this young man, at the age of twenty, was leading what I previously knew as the Integrity Knighthood—although considering the scope of the organization now, it was far larger than the knighthood from two centuries ago. I couldn't imagine the weight of the responsibilities on his shoulders.

It was strange to think about a man in his position spending his morning in this lonely, outcast mansion, preparing cofil tea and heating up honey pies for a stranger, but I still had more questions to ask him. Since I understood the source of the

Herlentz name now, I was more curious about how Eolyne had been brought into the family, but it was a delicate topic that was difficult to broach...

Sensing his chance while I was lost in thought, Eolyne said, "Well, you've heard plenty about me. Now it's your turn to speak, Kirito."

"Uh...w-well, as long as it's something I can answer...," I agreed, glancing around the tearoom. Fortunately, there was a large clock on the wall, but it was already 8:40. In the real world, Asuna and Alice would have arrived at the Roppongi office already and were preparing for their dive. I had to let them know I wouldn't be able to get to the Arabel mansion, but that they would have a ride to come meet me.

"...Before that, do you mind if I log...er, bounce out...I mean, return to the real world? I'll be back right away," I said timidly, earning me a very displeased look from the commander.

"You're not just saying that so you can disappear for three days again?"

"N-no, not at all. I'll return in five...no, three minutes."

"I suppose I cannot stop you; I have no means of keeping you here. Perhaps I will bake the second round of honey pies while I wait."

"That's a very strong incentive for me to come back," I said, grinning at Eolyne. Suddenly, another sharp pain ran through my chest. I'd traded jabs with Eugeo just like this hundreds of times. Despite the incredible similarity of his voice and tone, everything else that I learned about his background just reinforced the conclusion that he was a total stranger with no relation to Eugeo—just another individual in this era of the Underworld.

"...Well, I'll be right back," I said, waving briefly to stifle the pang. I input the log-out command with my left hand.

Until the bright light enveloped me and hid everything from sight, Eolyne maintained his faint smile and never once broke eye contact.

From the closest train station to Asuna's house, Miyanosaka Station on the Tokyu-Setagaya Line, to Rath's office in Roppongi, the commute was troublesome, if not quite as chaotic as getting to the returnee school. The shortest route required getting off the Setagaya Line at Sangenjaya Station to transfer to the Tokyu–Den-en-toshi Line, then changing to the Oedo Line at Aoyama-Itchome Station, and finally getting off at Roppongi Station. And the Oedo Line's Roppongi Station was the deepest subway station in Japan; it took over five minutes just to get up to the surface from there.

When her brother was a student and would complain, "If only there was a line that went straight from Shibuya to Roppongi or Azabu," she would snap, "Maybe you should stop going out at night." Little did she know that she, too, would make the very same wish, years later. As she stood in the largely empty Saturday-morning train, gently rocking as it traveled along the rails, she decided that the next time she went to Rath's office, she would try taking a bus from Shibuya Station instead. This thought was running through her mind when she noticed that there was a Kamura commercial running on the train's digital screen inside the car.

As the video cut between different images of smiling people of all ages wearing Augmas, she imagined for an instant that she had just seen Shikimi Kamura among them. But there was no way a member of the Kamura family would appear in their own commercial. She closed her eyelids and tried to banish the phantom smile from her mind but couldn't stop her thoughts from traveling back to the recent past.

During lunch period yesterday, Asuna had waited for Shikimi in the hallway, intent on fulfilling her promise to eat lunch with the girl this time. But after five minutes of valuable lunch period time, there was no sign of her. Asuna tried going to Shikimi's classroom, and they stated that she was absent today.

They hadn't exchanged contact information, so she knew Shikimi hadn't intentionally left her hanging, and of course the girl had every right to be absent due to physical distress or personal matters, just like anyone else. Still, Asuna couldn't help but feel something was strange about her absence. If she had to describe it, it was like Shikimi Kamuro's detailed, perfectionist life road map had been thrown astray by unforeseen factors.

But she was overthinking things. On Monday, Shikimi would come to see Asuna again, apologize for her absence, and invite her to lunch once more. And until that moment, Asuna needed to get a firm grip on her emotions so she wasn't rattled for no good reason again.

Everyone had their own path through life. Shikimi chose to go from Eterna Girls' Academy to a college overseas so she could build a dazzling future as the heir to the Kamura Company, and Asuna had her own path to travel. It was a path with Kirito, attempting to forge harmony between the real world and the Underworld, between humans and artificial fluctlights—a difficult but very worthwhile path.

There was no telling how many years it would take. She might not achieve it while she was still alive. But if so, that was simply her fate. It was a fate that had been determined for her the moment she put on the NerveGear and found herself trapped in a gigantic floating castle, a fate that she couldn't give to anyone else. Her extreme struggles until the early hours of the morning in *Unital Ring* each night and the dive she was about to undergo into the Underworld weren't simple detours. Shikimi might not understand or have an iota of interest in VRMMOs, but there was no reason to be ashamed of that. If the girl asked what Asuna did on her days off while they chatted over lunch, she would answer honestly. If Shikimi decided that it made Asuna not worth fraternizing with, that was better than pretending to get along with her based on a lie.

Isn't that right, Yuuki?

The thought of her dearly departed friend caused Asuna's eyes to shoot open. It was the very moment that the train car slid into Roppongi Station.

―∿∿―

I dived back in, ten seconds before hitting the three-minute mark I promised Eolyne, and was promptly met with a sweet, bracing scent.

As though perfectly timed for the moment I opened my eyes, a tray with a steaming, fresh-baked honey pie landed on the table. A voice said, with no small surprise, "Oh, you're back right on time."

"…What would you have done with this pie if I was late?" I asked, looking up.

The pilot commander wore a bemused smile below his face mask. "I would have fed you a cold pie, of course. You can only reheat a frozen honey pie once. Try it again, and it'll turn hard as a rock."

"…Good to know. I'm glad I made it in time," I said with relief. Eolyne sat down on my right, so I asked, "Um…do you have more frozen honey pies?"

"I do. Are you really that hungry?"

I was hungry enough that I could eat another ten of these delicious pies, but I wasn't asking for my own sake.

"No, I was hoping to give some to my friends, who should be arriving soon," I said, thinking of Asuna and Alice, whom I'd seen at the Roppongi office's STL room during my two minutes and fifty seconds back in the real world.

Eolyne's head bobbed. "Ah yes, I see. Don't worry about that. I've got another twenty or so in the freezer."

"Freezer…" I couldn't help but be taken aback; it was a familiar word in the real world, but I'd never heard it spoken before in the Underworld. "Are you chilling them with one of those coolers?" I asked, using the name of the device Phercy had mentioned.

But Eolyne shook his head. "No. This is an old building…Placing all the piping necessary for a cooler like the kind in Centoria would require so much work, the entire building would need to be rebuilt."

"How old are we talking about, actually?"

"I'd say it's easily three hundred years old. It was originally a villa in the private holdings of the imperial family of Norlangarth."

"Three hund...," I repeated, then realized that *that* wasn't the part to gawk at. Why was Eolyne using a villa belonging to the imperial family like his own private property? Unless...

"Wait...Were you from the Norlangarth imperial bloodline...?" I whispered, hushed.

Eolyne looked stunned for a moment, then burst into laughter. "Ha-ha-ha...Is that what you think? Well, I guess I can see why you might interpret what I said that way...Sadly, the answer is no." His chuckles subsided, and he took a sip of the fresh cup of cofil tea he'd prepared. "I wasn't born to such a prestigious family. Just the opposite, in fact."

"Opposite?"

"That's another story we can discuss later. You were asking about the freezer," Eolyne said, yanking the conversation back on track. He lifted his pointer finger. "As I said, we can't install large sealed canisters, so we use stand-alone freezers and ovens here. You don't have to get the pipes installed, but it means you have to recharge the frost and heat elements on your own."

A pale-blue light appeared on the tip of his finger. He extended his middle finger next, which generated a red point of light. Generating elements without a spoken command required a considerable amount of Incarnation power, and generating frost and heat elements at the same time, then holding them in the air, was an act of phenomenal skill.

Holding the two elements just an inch apart caused the heat and chill to mix, creating a trail of steam as the dots shrank and finally disappeared after ten seconds. As he blew on his fingertips to dispel the lingering steam, I stared at Eolyne and said the first thing that came to my mind.

"If you can do that…won't you get detected by those Incarnameter things? What if the city guard sends a car after you?"

"Anything as minor as generating elements won't be picked up unless you're in the same room as the device," he said.

"O-ohhh…"

I held out my fingers to do the same, but Eolyne squeezed them shut.

"You are the exception, Kirito. Your Incarnation power is off the charts, and that means that even tiny actions you take will cause massive Incarnate waves."

"I-Incarnate waves?"

"They're like ripples in space that the Incarnameter detects," he explained, then let go of my fingers and sank back down into the sofa. "And now I think we have reached the purpose of this conversation. Earlier, before you returned to the real world, I said that it would be your turn to speak next."

"Y…you did," I agreed.

The pilot commander fixed me with a stare through his mask. As though declaring that he was done making long, winding detours, he asked me a question that could not have been more direct.

"Star King Kirito, what is the reason that you have come back to the Underworld at this particular time?"

"……"

Eolyne would know if I tried to fool him, and any passing trust I'd built up through our interactions would easily evaporate into thin air, I could sense.

So I took a deep breath and opened my mouth to speak. "First of all…as I've said many times, I have no recognition or memory of being the Star King of this place. So if what you want from me is information that the Star King would know, I cannot help you."

"…Right," Eolyne said, brushing away a strand of wavy hair that fell in front of his mask. "I understand that. But earlier,

Kirito, you asked why I thought you were the Star King, when his name has been removed from all records, didn't you?"

"I did ask that."

"The answer is simple. The name has only been hidden, not lost. Though their numbers are few, there *are* still a few people alive who know the names of Star King Kirito and Star Queen Asuna. I am one of them."

"......I see."

If he was bringing up Asuna's name, too, then there was no point in denying it any longer. I wasn't interested in fully accepting this role, but assuming it was true that I'd once held the role of Star King, I could only pray that I hadn't decided on the title myself.

"Well, setting aside the matter of the Star King for the moment," I said, pantomiming placing an invisible object in empty space off to the left, "the reason I returned to the Underworld can be broadly split into two parts. One is to discover the identity and purpose of someone who has slipped into this world, who is not me nor my two companions."

"......"

Eolyne's mouth tightened just a bit, but he motioned for me to continue.

"And the other reason...is to bring back to life someone who is supposedly in a state of deep freeze in Central Cathedral."

Just in case, I chose not to mention Selka's name or the exact place where she was resting, but Eolyne seemed to recognize what I was talking about. He mulled it over, nodding to himself.

"......Yes, I see. Both of these answers were not what I expected, but neither are outside of the bounds of my responsibilities or creed. As the commander of the Integrity Pilothood, I believe I will be able to help with both of them."

"And the price....?" I asked, assuming he wouldn't offer for free.

Eolyne leaned forward, and in as quiet a voice as he could possibly produce, whispered, "I want you to help me, too."

Behind the thin glass lenses of the eyeholes in his mask, I could sense a powerful determination in those jade-green eyes. I nodded, my chin practically compelled beyond my discretion, but paused in the act.

"As long as it is within my ability and creed."

"Heh…" He chuckled. "That shouldn't be a problem. In fact…I have a feeling that your goals and my request are at least somewhat overlapping."

"What do you mean? What is your request…?"

"I want you to go to Admina with me," he said casually, a statement that I did not understand at first. Where was Admina, again…? And then I remembered.

"H-huh?! Admina, like…the *planet* Admina?!" I yelped, pointing at the ceiling of the tearoom—and past it, to the sky and to outer space beyond.

Eolyne just grinned and said, "That's right."

10

At nine thirty AM on October 3rd, 2026 AD (December 7th, Stellar Year 582), a new mechamobile arrived at the mansion in the woods, and Eolyne and I waited at the entrance hall to greet its passengers, Asuna and Alice.

I'd told them everything I could beforehand about the mysterious Integrity Pilot commander and requested that they allow me to handle anything involving his resemblance to Eugeo.

Asuna had never met Eugeo to begin with—only glimpsed visions of him in the fluctlight shard that dwelled inside the Blue Rose Sword—so her introduction and handshake were perfectly natural, but Alice could not hide the shock on her face.

Then again, shaking hands with Star Queen Asuna and the legendary Osmanthus Knight Alice was also a nerve-racking experience for Eolyne. It made me wonder, disgruntled, why he was so calm and steady with me, but I decided not to follow that up.

Back in the upstairs tearoom, Eolyne serve the two women their share of hot honey pies and cofil tea. They were delighted, of course, and Asuna wanted to know the recipe. Even worldly Eolyne did not know the answer, however, so we made vague plans to one day visit the actual Jumping Deer in North Centoria.

Before we could do that, however, we needed to decide on our plan for the near future.

Right as the women finished eating their pies, I asked Eolyne again for the reason that he wanted me to accompany him to the planet Admina. The pilot commander took a sip of cofil tea with cream and gave me an answer that shocked me even more than the original suggestion.

"The government of Admina, or perhaps its military command, is suspected of concocting plans to rebel against the Stellar Unification Council."

"...R-rebel?"

The three of us on the long sofa shared a look of shock. Choosing my words very carefully, I asked, "But...is that even possible in the Underworld? It's encoded in law that the Unification Council is the highest governing body of all, right?"

"Of course. It's written in the book of Stellar Law, Article One, Section Two. And as I'm sure you know, Underworlders do not break the law as a fundamental rule. In fact, they *cannot* break it."

"Then why are they suspected of rebellion?" Alice asked.

Eolyne straightened just a bit, and his answer to her was more properly spoken. "It is a rather complex subject, I'm afraid...Lady Alice, how well versed are you on the subject of dragoncraft?"

"Those are the steel dragons that Stica and Laurannei were riding...what they call airplanes in the real world...Or is it jet fighters?"

"Air-plains...jitt fighters," repeated Eolyne, grappling with the unfamiliar words. "I see. Well, at the moment, there are regular flights of large passenger and freight dragoncraft between the planet Cardina and its companion Admina. So in the style of the real world, you would call them...transport 'airplanes'?"

"Or passenger planes, maybe," Asuna pointed out.

The commander grimaced. "Then I shall call them that. The time it takes a passenger plane to fly from Cardina to Admina is about six hours. Theoretically, then, you could make two cycles in a single day. But until a month and a half ago, we could only fly once every week. Do you know why that is?"

Asuna and Alice looked befuddled, but the mention of that timeframe was familiar to me. That was around the time that the three of us first visited the later Underworld, two hundred years after our original timeline.

"...Was it that space monster? The...Abyssal Horror?"

"Yes. But we call it a spacebeast," said Eolyne, a little shorter with me. I didn't mind it, though, and the girls didn't seem to notice.

"For a long time—since before Admina was even discovered—the Abyssal Horror has flown between our two planets at a specific speed, along a specific route. If spotted and attacked, even the most heavily armed dragoncraft stands no chance. In fact, very long ago, a passenger plane headed to Admina was destroyed, killing many on board. According to legend, it was vanquished three times by the Star King, but in each case, a small piece of it escaped into the darkness of space, only to return in a fully regenerated form..."

We nodded our heads in understanding.

"Yes, we thought Asuna's meteor drop blew it to pieces, but those bits just wriggled away like bugs, trying to escape. After that, Alice's Memory Release art eliminated every last one, as I recall," I said, glancing over at the Integrity Knight on my left.

She had worn a brown cloak when getting out of the mechamobile, but she had taken it off since then, revealing her full suit of golden armor. Her divine weapon, the Osmanthus Blade, along with Asuna's GM weapon, Radiant Light, and my Night-Sky Blade and Blue Rose Sword were all brought inside in a heavy-duty leather bag that was now resting on the floor of the tearoom. But even without her sword at her side, the knight's pristine, noble aura was completely untarnished.

Alice's blue eyes caught mine in a glare. "Are you doubting my technique? I destroyed every last piece of that monster."

"N-no, no, I'm not doubting you. But it's just kind of a trope that there's always one of those things that escapes by hiding somewhere you'd never expect...like on the underside of your armor, say..."

"So you *are* doubting me!" Alice snapped.

"Ugh, don't be gross!" scolded Asuna.

Eolyne wore a strangely conflicted look on his face—probably because his mental images of the Star Queen and the Osmanthus Knight were being overwritten somewhat—but he did offer me a life preserver.

"Have no fear, my ladies. In times past, the Abyssal Horror returned in full after a single month, but it has now been a month and half, with no sign of it. The battle itself is top secret, so this information is classified, but after much strict observation, the Integrity Pilothood has concluded that the dreaded spacebeast is no more."

"Y-yeah. So we're all good here. Great news," I said, nodding eagerly and reaching for the pot on the table. I refilled Asuna's, Alice's, and even Eolyne's cup with more cofil tea.

"So...how does the ol' AH tie in to this rebellion talk?" I asked, earning an annoyed look from Eolyne at my lazy abbreviation.

"The Abyssal Horror was considered the greatest scourge in all of the Underworld," he explained, "so there is no way for us to express the depth of our gratitude for eliminating it. But the truth is: That fight should never have happened."

"...Meaning?"

"I just told you that the Abyssal Horror flew around the two planets, following a specific speed and route, but this is a living thing we're talking about. Because it would alter its orbit on rare occasions, Cardina and Admina each built specific observation centers, using enormous telescopes to track the spacebeast and keep a firm grasp on its location before authorizing any dragoncraft to fly. A month and a half ago, Pilot Arabel and Pilot Schtrinen left Cardina based on information from Admina that the Abyssal Horror was traveling on the far side of the planet. There should have been no chance that they would encounter the spacebeast during a three-hour flight," he said, finishing close to a whisper.

Asuna was the first to react. "Meaning…that either the Abyssal Horror moved with incredible speed or Admina's information was wrong…?"

"Yes, one of the two…But the former is not possible. The Abyssal Horror moves very slowly when it is not attacking a dragoncraft and the people inside, so it's simply unthinkable that it would move from the far side of Admina to the place where it encountered the pilots in less than an hour. And for the latter to be true, an experienced observer would have to mistake that massive beast's shadow for some other object. And that is hard to believe…"

"Meaning that they might have intentionally sent bad information," Alice pointed out bluntly. Eolyne seemed to tense briefly.

"Yes, I…I suspect that may be the case."

"W-wait just a minute," I said, envisioning the young faces of Stica and Laurannei. "Are you saying that someone tried to get the Abyssal Horror to attack those two…and kill them?"

"That would be the case, if so," said Eolyne with a sigh. He'd been sitting directly upright but now leaned against the back cushion of the sofa. "I'll explain in further detail later, but in fact, there are other cases of suspected sabotage and destruction of Cardina Space Force assets. If they are attempting to weaken our overall military strength, we must assume that it is because they intend to rebel against us. But I simply cannot believe that the director of Admina's government or the commander of Admina's base would be involved in such a thing…They are both great figures whom I've known since I was a child."

"…Is it not possible for great people with a great cause to stage a rebellion?" I asked, hesitating slightly.

Eolyne murmured, "In the same way that you started a rebellion against the Axiom Church, long ago?"

"……"

I held my breath for a bit longer than usual but shook my head. "No. I didn't fight the church for some great cause. It was for myself…and for my partner."

I fought to fulfill Eugeo's wish to free Alice Zuberg from the

Axiom Church's grasp and take her back to Rulid. But I failed at that, and Eugeo lost his life in the ultimate battle against Administrator.

Eugeo's fluctlight was destroyed, along with a piece of the young Alice's fluctlight, on the top floor of Central Cathedral. *So why do you have his hair and voice and demeanor, Eolyne?*

Once again, I had to grit my teeth not to give in to the urge to ask this question, and it was Alice who spoke instead.

"Eolyne Herlentz: To you, the battle between Kirito and the Axiom Church might be ancient history, but for Kirito, it happened only months ago. It should not be spoken of lightly by one who is not in full possession of the details."

"...I humbly apologize, Lady Alice," he said immediately, giving me a nod as well. "Sorry about that, Kirito. One day I would like to know the truth about your fight against the Axiom Church...But let us speak only about what is necessary now. It is true that great people can lead rebellions. But such things require a valid reason to break Stellar Law. Say, if Cardina was tormenting the people of Admina, for example."

"And that's not happening?"

"Not in the slightest. The Star King created many laws protecting Admina, to prevent such a thing from occurring. So Admina should have no reason to attack Cardina. But...when you mentioned that someone from your real world had infiltrated the Underworld, it made me think. Perhaps this is just the first glimmer of a new Otherworld War."

"...!!"

All three of us sucked in a sharp breath.

Asuna was the first to react. She turned to Eolyne, her pearl-white armor sliding the tiniest bit, and asked, "You think that the intruder from the real world is fomenting discord...trying to start a war between Cardina and Admina?"

"The God of Darkness, Vecta, who caused the old Otherworld War was a real-worlder, wasn't he? So it's not so far-fetched that the same thing could happen again."

His logic was sound. But Stica and Laurannei were attacked by the Abyssal Horror on the very same day that we dived into the Stellar Calendar era of the Underworld. If someone from our world manipulated things to set that up, they would have to have infiltrated the Underworld before we went in.

Was that even possible? And if so, either that person had some connection to Akihiko Kayaba, or perhaps…

I had to forcefully stop myself from thinking any further about it.

"And you want to go to Admina to learn more about this," I concluded.

"That's right," said Eolyne, adding impossibly, "but we can't use a dragoncraft."

"…Huh?"

"In order for us to roam freely in Admina, we must secretly infiltrate the planet. But flying between planets with Integrity Pilot or space force crafts requires advance authorization from the Admina government, and riding on a large transport dragoncraft requires a citizen number. Both of these will be very difficult to fake."

"Can't we just fly there secretly, without a permit?"

"If even a single dragoncraft disappears from the base hangar, it will turn into a huge emergency involving the Unification Council. It's not like taking a mechamobile."

"That makes sense…," I admitted, crestfallen. But then I realized that something was wrong here. It was the commander's wish to go to Admina in the first place. "How *were* you planning to get to Admina, then?"

Without batting an eye, Eolyne said, "There are two methods. The first is for you to use Incarnation to transport me, Lady Asuna, and Lady Alice."

"H…huh?! You want to fly to another planet…without a craft? Just floating out there?!"

"When you rescued the two pilots, they said you were flying freely through space."

"Y-yeah, that's true, but..."

Unlike in the real world, outer space in the Underworld was not a vacuum. As I'd thought about when pondering Mutasina's suffocation magic, the concepts of vacuum and non-vacuum didn't exist in the virtual world. So while space here was dark and cold and without gravity, you could still breathe and talk. You could probably use wind element flight, too, so it was hypothetically possible to travel from planet to planet using Incarnation, but...

"But that's just going to make those Incarnation waves, right? I assume Admina's got at least one or two Incarnameters..."

"Yes, one or two hundred, I'd say. Someday, you'll need to learn Incarnation-Hiding Incarnation...But even the Star King will take some time to do that. So I think we'll use the second method instead."

"And that is...?"

"Very simple. Simply use a dragoncraft that no one will notice is missing."

We sat in aghast silence as Eolyne raised his hand and gestured toward the south wall of the tearoom—the direction of Centoria.

"In the sealed-off upper floors of Central Cathedral, the Star King's personal dragoncraft, the X'rphan Mk. 13, should still be stored and operational. With that, as long as we can hide the fact that it's left the tower, the higher-ups at the Unification Council won't notice."

The boldness of the idea was shocking enough, but even more shocking was the name of the dragoncraft. I glanced to my left, over Alice to Asuna, who was wide-eyed herself.

X'rphan was the name of a field boss on the fifty-fifth floor of Aincrad—not the new version installed in *ALO*, but the original from *SAO*. The full name was X'rphan the White Wyrm. As the name suggested, it was a pure-white dragon, which made it a suitable name for a dragoncraft...Yet that all but confirmed that the Star King was familiar with *Sword Art Online*.

No, not now! Later! I told myself, looking back at Eolyne. "That does sound more realistic than flying there with Incarnation. But can we get into where it's sealed away? What kind of seal are we talking about, actually?"

"Aside from the great stairs of Central Cathedral, there is an automated platform that can move from the first to the seventy-ninth floor. But if you take it to the eightieth floor, which it normally cannot be directed to do, there is a huge door right past the landing. Even the Stellar Unification Council is forbidden from approaching that door. I expect that it is heavily locked."

"……"

This time, I stared at Alice. The golden knight's eyes were trained on a single point in space.

I was certain that those eyes were gazing directly at her sister, Selka, who was trapped in a deep sleep on the eightieth floor of the cathedral. Despite considering her awakening my top-priority mission, I hadn't a clue of how we were going to get into the structure, but now there was an unexpected light at the end of the tunnel. I was certain that Alice was currently upswelling with a huge amount of hope—and just a tiny bit of unease.

Eolyne could clearly sense something from our reactions. He murmured, "I see…So that person you mentioned being in deep freeze in the cathedral has something to do with Lady Alice, I presume?"

Well, there was no point trying to pretend otherwise now. I admitted, "Yeah…Do you know anything about that?"

"I've certainly never been as high as the eightieth floor, you understand…All I've been told is that the ancient Integrity Knights are sealed at the top of Central Cathedral, and the Star King's dragoncraft is there as well. Also…"

He hesitated, then decided to go ahead, dropping his voice to a whisper.

"…One of the Crystal Panels, of which there are only three in the Underworld, is installed on the top floor. That's all."

It was clear what Eolyne was talking about: the system console for manipulating the Underworld itself.

A thought occurred to me. If we used that, couldn't we find

out about the intruder directly, without having to travel all the way to Admina? But the console was completely locked out at the beginning of the maximum acceleration phase, turning it into nothing but an actual crystal panel. The acceleration was long over, but if we were going to use it again, we'd probably have to perform a reset from the control room of the *Ocean Turtle*...

But we would know all these things once we were there. The first destination, of course, being the place where Selka rested.

Sensing that I'd asked everything I needed to, I placed my hands on my lap and leaned forward. "Well, if that's all settled, let's go back to Centoria. Will another mechamobile come for us?"

Yet again, Eolyne put on an uncomfortable, chagrined smile. "You're rather impatient, aren't you? I was expecting the legendary Star King to be more...relaxed about things."

Before I could say anything, Asuna and Alice chimed in.

"Exactly!"

"I agree."

Eolyne placed a voice call to somewhere—or voice transponder, or whatever they called it here—and before long, I could hear the rumble of an engine in the front approach of the mansion.

We descended the stairs, the commander taking the lead. I carried the large brown bag; with four divine weapons inside, it was incredibly heavy.

At Eolyne's recommendation, Asuna and Alice changed out of their goddess and Integrity Knight armor and into standard Integrity Pilot uniforms. Alice, in particular, was hesitant to leave her trusty armor behind, but at Eolyne's insistence that no one could enter the mansion without his authorization, and his offer to lock the room in which the armor was stored, she begrudgingly agreed to play along.

But in fact, the navy-blue uniform and cap that Stica and Laurannei wore looked very good on both Asuna and Alice, and I actually applauded when they emerged from their changing room.

Alice, her face red, asked, "Aren't you going to change, too?" But according to the commander, my clothes were already fairly standard design for the Underworld and wouldn't draw any extra attention on the street.

Alice had removed her golden armor, but she still wore a firm, rectangular belt pack. Inside were two large eggs, bigger than standard chicken eggs. They were the eggs of her dragon, Amayori, and its big brother, Takiguri, which I had rewound to a pre-hatched state with Incarnation.

She probably wished they would hatch so she could raise them, but that was a difficult ask at this point in time. She couldn't be logged in to the Underworld at all times, which meant she'd need to leave them in the care of someone trustworthy—and there were very few people in this age who had experience raising dragons, I was sure.

We crossed the entrance hall and headed outside, where we were promptly greeted by two cheery voices accompanied by the clicking of boot heels snapping into place.

""We've come with your ride!""

Saluting us at the bottom of the porch were two girls dressed in the uniform and cap of the Integrity Pilothood: Stica Schtrinen and Laurannei Arabel. Their arrival was a total surprise to me.

"Huh?" I squawked. "I assumed you were doing your real jobs today..."

"They ought to be." Eolyne sighed, walking beside me. "At their young ages, they're the aces of the Blue Rose Company. Ordinarily, they're as busy barracudas, between training new operators and testing experimental dragoncraft; they shouldn't be acting as chauffeurs, but they insisted, so..."

If there's no sea in the Underworld, how does he know what a barracuda is...?

But that wasn't worth wondering about; it was the mention of the Blue Rose Company. Operator Second Class Lagi Quint had said he was in the Cattleya Company, which meant that the different companies of the Integrity Pilots were named after flowers—and so-called sacred flowers, at that. But why was it Blue Rose instead of just Rose?

I made a mental note to ask Eolyne about that later. Meanwhile, the girls lowered their salutes and rushed over to us.

"Lady Alice, Lady Asuna, Sir Kirito, it's so good to see you!"

"I'm so happy we got the chance to meet again!"

They were all radiant smiles. Alice and Asuna gave them warm hugs. I didn't have the boldness to do the same, so I settled for handshakes. When Laurannei noticed the large bag I was carrying, she held out both hands and said, "I'll carry your bag to the car!"

"Don't worry; I'll do it. This thing's heavy."

"Please, it's my duty!" she insisted, pulling the bag out of my hand, then yelped, "*Ullgh!*"

I didn't blame her. There were four full-sized swords in the bag, each one close to class-50 in priority. Asuna and Alice had to take it out of the car together, so there was no way one of the girls could do it alone, even if she was an ace pilot.

I very nearly used Incarnation to help hold it up, but Laurannei's downward slump stopped just before the bottom of the bag touched the ground, and she held it there. Gritting her teeth, face turning red, she puffed, "*Hrrrrgh,*" and slowly, very slowly, lifted the huge bag higher.

Since I was too stunned to do anything but stare, Asuna and Alice tried to help her, but the girl refused their help. She looked at her partner and grunted through gritted teeth, "S...Sti... H-help me..."

Stica was already grabbing one of the straps. She and Laurannei took one each to share the load, and now they were both straining and groaning, "*Frrhngh...*"

Somehow, they managed to straighten upright and hauled the bag over to the vehicle, panting "One-two, one-two" in rhythm. If they were able to carry four divine weapons between the two of them, that meant they could easily have the Object Control level individually to equip one of them.

I watched them go, feeling more than a little stunned by this realization, and once they seemed out of earshot, I whispered to Eolyne, "How far along are they, actually?"

"Fifteen, if I recall."

I was asking about their authority level, but Eolyne answered with their age. That number, too, was shocking.

"Fifteen…?! That's normally the age when people would be *starting* at Swordcraft Academy. How is their authority level so high…?"

"That is because the Arabel and Schtrinen families are the most prestigious there can be," Eolyne said cryptically, patting me on the back. "Come, let's get in. I'd like to have lunch in Centoria, wouldn't you?"

11

The mechamobile Laurannei drove wasn't a large black sedan like the one I took in, but a well-used white van. The interior and comfort level were very...practical, and the trip down the little cobbled road was quite noisy.

Four people couldn't ride in the back seat of the sedan, and we were trying to keep a lower profile, but I couldn't deny that I was a little disappointed I wouldn't get to enjoy that smooth, luxurious ride again. On the lightly cushioned right seat of the third row, I told myself that I was going to ask his lordship the commander for a chance to drive the black one sometime.

In the middle row, Alice lamented to Asuna, "The first time I saw the roads of the real world, with the huge crowds of automobiles driving many times the speed of a horse-drawn carriage, I felt that I had come to a greatly advanced world, even if it did make me dizzy with how frenetic it was. And now there are metal carriages like this in the Underworld, too..."

"On the other hand, the mechamobiles here don't produce harmful pollution like the autos over there," I said, in an odd attempt to be helpful.

Eolyne, however, was not in the same state of mind. "But because of all the mechamobiles and coolers, scarcity of spatial resources is becoming a real problem. In fact, this summer, we had three separate instances of all the machines that run off of eternal elements shutting down together. They said it was because of many homes running their cooling simultaneously in the middle of the night, when Solus cannot provide more spatial power."

I recalled that little Phercy had said the same thing. "But summer in Centoria isn't so bad that you need to use cooling, is it?" I asked, the first thing that came to my mind. "We didn't have coolers back at Swordcraft Academy's dorms, of course, and it was easy to sleep at night…"

"While they are within range of common households now, coolers are still an expensive item to own. It's only human nature to want to use something that costs you dearly to acquire," Eolyne explained, which made sense to me.

Next, Asuna asked, "Does Centoria have power charges…? Or spatial resource charges, I guess?"

"Spatial resource charges…? Oh…you mean money that you spend to use those resources? No, of course not. Spatial resources are brought to us by nature, just like water and wind."

"In the real world, people pay money to use water, too," Alice informed him.

"Oh my," he replied, looking at us with pity. "But…that might be a solution, I suppose. If we created a system to levy costs commensurate with the amount of resources used, we could curtail overuse of cooling. The problem would be how to measure the usage…"

The pilot commander and the council member devolved into muttering, so I hastened to cut him off.

"W-well, we can certainly discuss that another time."

I really didn't want to create a situation, much later in time, where the Underworld's school textbooks contained the historical fact that it was a real-worlder named Kirito who introduced the concept of charging money for water and spatial power. That was not a reputation I wanted.

"More importantly, um…How high of a Perfect Weapon

Control authority do you need to enter the Integrity Pilots?" I asked, recalling the question I meant to bring up earlier.

Eolyne shrugged. "There's no actual requirement that you need to fulfill a certain value. First, you achieve high marks at school, then preferably earn a prize among the upper ranks of the Stellar Unification Combat Tournament, then enter the space force or ground force as a potential officer, and if you show keen talent in that environment, you can be recommended to take the test to be a pilot," he explained smoothly, speaking up toward the front seat. "Stica, Laurannei, how old were you when you tied in the final of the Unification Tournament?"

"Twelve!" Stica responded from the passenger seat.

Laurannei, her hands on the steering wheel, added, "But I was the winner."

"Wha...? No, you weren't! If anything, I had *you* on the ropes."

"Is that how you say 'flailed around wildly'?"

"Grrrr!"

Their lighthearted bickering was very age appropriate, but if the Stellar Unification Combat Tournament was an expanded version of the Four-Empire Unification Tournament, being crowned co-champions at age twelve was beyond the level of genius. Not even the old Integrity Knights featured any talents that blossomed so early, as far as I knew.

In the back of my mind, I recalled the helpless smile on the face of Phercy Arabel—and his resignation over every aspect of his future.

He said he was only nine years old. His own sister triumphed at the greatest combat tournament in all of the Underworld when she was just three years older than that, but he couldn't even execute an ultimate technique yet. It was hard to imagine how much despair he must have felt about that vast discrepancy. I told myself that someday I'd make time to sit down with Phercy and get to the bottom of the mystery that tormented him.

"When I triumphed in the Unification Tournament, I was

sixteen," said Eolyne, loud enough for the whole car to hear. "I suppose that both of you have surpassed me, as swordsmen and as operators."

"N-no, sir! That's not true!" insisted Stica, pausing in her fight with Laurannei. "We don't even hold a candle to your transcendental swordfighting and piloting ability! You mustn't say things like that!"

Keeping her eyes on the road, Laurannei added, "That's right; it was just half a year ago that you faced us together—and easily handled us both. It will take us another ten years to surpass you."

"N-no, we'll *never* surpass him, Dummy Laura!"

"Actually, it's rude to insist that it must be impossible, Crybaby Sti."

In the row behind the bickering girls, Asuna and Alice laughed silently. Eolyne, meanwhile, just shook his head and sighed.

While they might look just like Ronie and Tiese, the quarreling was something that those girls never did, I couldn't help but notice. And while my mind was wandering, I asked the commander, "By the way, what's *your* authority level?"

"Huh...?"

Eolyne's mouth hung open with surprise, and when I looked at him, a revelation struck my brain like a bolt of lightning.

In Eolyne Herlentz's status pop-up—his Stacia Window—it would list not just his object control authority and system control authority, but also his human unit ID number.

And if Eolyne did happen to have some connection to Eugeo— if he just so happened to *be* the same person, missing his memory— then their ID numbers would match.

I would never forget it. He was NND7-6361, just six numbers off of mine, 6355. If that was the number that appeared in Eolyne's window, then...

He gave me an odd look, noticing how I had frozen in place. "Hmmm," he said, "I wonder how high it is...I don't normally pay attention to my own."

"…Then show me your Stacia Window," I said as casually as I could. It earned me another one of his chagrined smirks.

"Listen, Kirito, I don't know how things were two hundred years ago, but these days, the only people who insist on seeing others' windows are guards who've mistakenly inflated their own importance."

"Well…that was true back then, too…"

I had to fight a sudden urge to just grab Eolyne's hand and force him to do the gesture. I didn't know what to say.

"Tell you what. If you show me your window first, Kirito, I'll show you mine."

"……"

I held my breath at this unexpected turn of events. My stats? He was free to see however much he wanted; it didn't mean anything to me.

Awkwardly, I bobbed my head, praying that my voice would sound casual and natural. "Okay, let's do that, I guess. Here, I'll show you mine first."

I made an S-shape in the air with two fingers, then struck the back of my left hand with them. With a bell-like chime, a purple window appeared.

In the previous dive, I was forced to open it for the guards who'd come barging into the Arabel mansion, but I hadn't actually checked on my own authority level at the time. So I leaned in close, bumping heads with Eolyne so we could peer into the small rectangle.

"Ah…You've got a very low ID number, as I'd expect you would. I've never seen anyone in the six-thousands before."

The ID number NND7-6355 meant that I came from the NND7 area, which was in the far north of the realm, and that I was the six thousand three hundred and fifty-fifth person born there.

"The captain of the city guard said the same thing," I replied, focusing on the right side of the window.

In fact, I hadn't looked at these two values since around when I found the Integrity Knights at Central Cathedral. At the time, my OC (Object Control) level was around 50, and my SC (System Control) level was around 30. Maybe they'd gone up a bit…

But when I saw the actual values, my mouth made a weird little "*Ueih?*" sound.

There was no mistaking the numerals in the simple font. My OC authority was 29, and my SC authority was 07.

"I…I went down?! To twenty-nine and seven…," I said, aghast. I looked at my hand, but there was nothing written on it, of course.

I guessed pedestrian numbers like these would explain why the whiskered captain hadn't reacted to them. But everything else about it didn't sit right with me. There was no way I could equip both the Night-Sky Blade and Blue Rose Sword at the same time with those numbers. And was it really right that they could go down? The Abyssal Horror didn't have some level-draining ability, did it?

"Kirito…," Eolyne whispered.

Dejected, I said, "I dunno…I'm sorry about these numbers. This should make it clear that I'm not the Star King, though, right?"

"It's not that…Look here. Do you think that's a tiny '1' written there?"

"Huh? A tiny '1'…?"

Eolyne was pointing just to the left of the OC authority value on the Stacia Window. I leaned in closer and squinted.

Sure enough, between the square bracket around the value and the 2, there was what appeared to be a number 1, only half as large as the other numbers.

I shared a look with Eolyne, then glanced at the window again. "Wait…Are you saying that's three digits, not two? So it's not 29 and 7…it's 129 and 107?"

"Yes…I suppose so. I didn't know you could get over a hundred…," Eolyne stated with quiet awe. He stared me in the eyes and added, "But if anyone could do it, I suppose the legendary Star King could."

"………W-we don't know that yet," I said, feeling ashamed of how childish it sounded, and hastily closed the window. Anyway, whether it was two or three digits, my current authority level didn't matter.

"Okay, your turn now," I said, in what I hoped was a casual tone, but I couldn't keep the last word from quavering.

Eolyne didn't seem to notice or care and said, "Fine. But let me preface this by saying that I know my authority levels are nowhere near yours."

With a smooth, practiced motion, he drew an S with his right hand and tapped his left. There was another chime sound, and his Stacia Window appeared.

My eyes were drawn to the unit ID in the upper left: NCD1-13091.

It was not at all similar to Eugeo's unit ID, and I found myself gazing emptily at the number. After five seconds, or maybe ten, Eolyne said, just a bit peevishly, "You don't have to be *that* disappointed. I warned you that they weren't going to be close, didn't I?"

"Huh? Oh…"

I came back to my senses and looked at the right side. His OC was 62 and his SC was 58. Both were only half of my own, but by the standards I was used to two centuries ago, they were extremely high. It was higher than mine back then—*and* the Integrity Knights'.

"No, those numbers were incredible. I can see why you're the commander," I told him, despite the numbness in my brain.

Eolyne smirked once again. "Well, coming from you, it sounds sarcastic…But I thank you for the kind words," he murmured, closing his Stacia Window and leaning back into his chair. I faced forward and rested against the stiff seat back.

In the row ahead of us, Asuna and Alice were chatting pleasantly with the girls in the front. The mechamobile had already made its way back into Centoria, where expensive-looking cars were using the passing lane to zoom around us.

For an instant, I thought I saw flaxen hair in the passenger seat of a sedan and looked harder. But the car zipped past and was soon out of sight.

Just because his ID was different didn't mean I should draw any direct conclusions from it.

But maybe it was time to admit something. Like in the real world, perhaps the Underworld could produce twin strangers, too. Perhaps I was just seeking a miracle in the midst of coincidence, a miracle that would not happen.

"...What's the matter?"

The voice caused me to pull my eyes away from the window. That was when I felt that a single tear had tracked down my left cheek.

"Oh...it's nothing," I said, lifting my hand and brushing it away. The little droplet perched on my finger for a moment, then melted away into nothing.

On Eolyne's orders, Laurannei turned the white mechamobile left off the main street and into a parking lot in the corner of a busy commercial area.

He took us to a small but rather comfortable restaurant located in a quiet backstreet with little foot traffic. There were no other customers because it was too early for lunch. When the chef and waitress saw the Integrity Pilot uniforms, they greeted us warmly, and for the first time in a long time, I got to enjoy some North Centorian cooking. Eolyne paid the tab for six lunches, and I found it quite entertaining to see how self-conscious Alice felt about this, for some reason.

Back in the car, we returned to the main street. This time we took no detours but headed straight for the gigantic white tower directly ahead of us. Once we reached the tall walls around it, we turned left to circle around to the south gate.

In the days of the Axiom Church, even nobles and emperors could not enter Central Cathedral grounds, much less common people. But now the south gate was open, and the mechamobile rolled right through to the interior without so much as a security check.

Human and demi-human tourists alike were strolling leisurely throughout the garden, which still retained its old look. The mechamobile turned left down the road that traveled along the inside of the wall, until after a while, it turned right.

With a sudden shock, Alice exclaimed, "The dragon stables are gone!"

Indeed, the huge stables that existed on the western side of the tower two centuries ago had completely vanished, and a parking lot now stood where they had once been.

"What happened to the dragons?!" she asked, turning back in horror.

Anticipating this question, Eolyne said calmly, "According to our records, at the same time that the Integrity Knights were sealed away, half the dragons kept at Central Cathedral were returned to their habitat in Wesdarath, while the other half were sealed with the knights. Even today, many dragons live in their protected area in the western ranges of Wesdarath, in their natural way."

"Oh…I see," said Alice, her face softening. "But what exactly does this sealing mean? How does it work?"

"…I'm sorry, Lady Alice, but even I do not know. But as long as we get into the upper floors of the cathedral, everything should become clear."

"……Yes, I agree," she whispered, facing forward again.

A few seconds later, the car reached the back of the parking lot, did a quick and practiced turn, and backed perfectly into a spot.

It was just past eleven o'clock in the morning. Dr. Koujiro gave us a hard time limit to return again, this time at five in the afternoon. So we had six hours to work with, I calculated—and then finally realized a huge problem.

"Um…Eolyne," I called out to the commander, who had just gotten out of the car.

"What is it?"

"Um…I hate to bring this up so belatedly, but Asuna and Alice and I can't be in the Underworld past five in the evening again. We'll be able to come back tomorrow morning, most likely. But I'm guessing we won't reach Admina in another six hours, will we…?"

"Hmmm…" Eolyne glanced up at the top of Central Cathedral. "It depends on the time we leave and the capabilities of the X'rphan Mk. 13, but I think in terms of actual travel, we'll make it."

"W-wow, for real…?" I stammered, accidentally slipping into some language that was definitely not native to the Underworld. But this being a virtual world, there was no reason that the scale of outer space had to be the same as reality. Supposedly it was a six-hour flight one way with a passenger jet, so if Cardina and Admina were closer than I suspected, then maybe…But no, even still, there was no way we could complete the investigation of the intruder and make it back to Centoria in time.

I wanted to explain all this to him, but Eolyne spoke first. "I think we might be able to solve your stay limitations, however."

"Huh? Wh-what do you mean...?"

"I'll explain later," he promised, then walked over to the two girls, who were standing at attention along the left side of the mechamobile. "Well done, you two. I don't know when my task will be over, so you may return to the base for today."

Stica promptly straightened her back and remarked, "No, my lord, we will accompany you until your business is complete!"

Laurannei joined in. "We have permission to be out until the end of the day, so lateness is no concern!"

"Wh-what? Really?"

""Really!!""

Meanwhile, I pulled the bag of swords out of the luggage space. Asuna approached and whispered, "That's one area where they're just like Tiese and Ronie."

"Seriously...," I agreed.

On my right, Alice murmured, "Actually, I would say that they're much closer to you and Eugeo."

"Huh?"

"I think you two rubbed off on Ronie and Tiese, and that influence made its way down to these girls."

"..."

It seemed far-fetched, but I couldn't rule it out. When we were primary trainees at the academy, we argued in all kinds of obnoxious ways with our dorm supervisor, Miss Azurica. Although usually it was me doing the arguing and Eugeo getting caught in the backlash.

If Alice's idea was accurate, then the spirit of rebelliousness the girls were exhibiting against Eolyne came from me. On the inside, I gave the harried commander a silent "Sorry about that." Eventually, however, Eolyne gave in, and the three of them came our way.

"Well, let's go," he said, walking toward the garage exit with the two pilots. We exchanged secret smiles and hurried after them.

Of course, Central Cathedral itself wasn't open to the public; a menacing security gate loomed over the entrance to the building.

Eolyne approached the gate, where guards stood in white uniforms with thin swords hanging from their belts. He pulled what looked like an identification card from beneath his cloak and showed it to the worker inside the booth. For a moment, I wondered if the Integrity Pilot commander and Steller Unification Council member didn't get in on sight because of the mask. But the worker checked his identification diligently, so it seemed that this was the ordinary treatment.

I started to worry that this meant we'd be asked for identification next, but the Integrity Pilot uniforms did the trick. Stica, Laurannei, Alice, and Asuna were allowed to pass through the gate without question. As the only one wearing a different uniform, I earned some glares from the guards, but they did not ask me to show them my bag or stop me from passing through.

We crossed the large entrance area, and I only allowed myself to exhale once we were a good distance away from the gate. Eolyne whispered, "I'm sorry about that, Kirito."

"F-for what…?"

"I explained that you were my luggage-carrying servant. It was the only way to get you through."

"Oh, I see. Well, it's way better than being treated like the Star King…," I insisted.

"Let's hurry," said Alice. Her voice was just a bit ragged.

I couldn't blame her for feeling hasty. The moment she'd been waiting on for months was nearly within her grasp.

"Very well. Come this way," said Eolyne, quickly crossing the empty hall. Alice and Asuna proceeded behind him, with Stica, Laurannei, and me in the rear.

The great hall on the first floor of the cathedral still featured the marble walls and pillars I remembered, but the furnishings were quite different. Most attention-grabbing were the massive tapestries that hung from each of the four walls. The mark on them, blue on white, was the Stellar Unification Council's logo, symbolizing Solus, Cardina, and Admina. Near the tip, the small symbol of two swords and two types of flowers arranged in a diamond shape was the insignia of the Star King, I was told.

The great stairs at the other end of the entrance hall were split into right and left sides, with a small fountain trickling pleasantly a little ways before them. I felt as though there had originally been just one staircase and no fountain, but I supposed that in the course of two hundred years, some renovations were bound to happen.

After circling around the rather aged marble fountain, I saw that there were three doors on the far wall, which I took to be elevators.

Two centuries ago, Central Cathedral had an elevator—which was called the levitation shaft—but it only connected the fiftieth to eightieth floors, and in order to get up to the fiftieth floor, you had to take the stairs. The levitation shaft was operated manually by a girl called the Operator. So did they…just increase the number of operators?

But even if that was the case, they would at least be taking shifts, unlike before. In fact, I prayed that it was so as we walked up to the doors, and Stica pressed a round button on the wall. The center door slid open to both sides, and thankfully, the interior was empty.

Over the centuries, they had automated the elevator. I thanked whoever had kick-started that process as I followed the other five in.

Originally, the levitating platform had been circular, but it was now a square, like in the real world. There was still room to spare, even with six of us riding it. The doors closed with a faint mechanical rattle. Next to them was a panel with three rows of metal buttons.

The numbers on the buttons went from one to seventy-nine. As Eolyne said, there was no button to take us to the eightieth floor.

"So…what now?" I asked quietly.

Eolyne fixed me with a look. "I was thinking that maybe something would happen if you got on…"

"I don't know why you would think that…"

I looked around the box, but nothing noteworthy was happening. If we kept waiting for something to happen, someone else was bound to get into the elevator with us.

"Um…Maybe we should go up to the seventy-ninth floor," I suggested, reaching for the top button—but held my finger back before I pressed it.

"What is it?" asked Asuna.

"I don't know…," I murmured, staring at the control panel. The numbers started at the bottom with 1-2-3, then 4-5-6. By that pattern, the top row should be 76-77-78, with 79 left over on its own.

But on the top row of the panel, there was only 78 and 79, side by side. That was because the bottom row had just 1 and 2, before resuming with three each: 3-4-5, 6-7-8, and so on.

"Eolyne…do the other elevators—er, levitating platforms—have the same button arrangement?" I asked.

The commander's round hat bobbed. "We call them levitators, actually. Hmm…I'm not sure. I've never really paid attention to that."

"I'll go and see!"

"Me too!"

Stica and Laurannei opened the door and bolted out. After ten seconds, they came back and reported the results as soon as the door was closed again.

"The right levitator only has the seventy-ninth button on the top row!"

"Same for the left levitator!"

"Thank you both," I said, examining the panel once more. Only the middle box had a different button layout. Was that a consequence of the way they were made—or was it done that way by design?

I reached out and touched the metal plate to the right of where the 79 button sat.

"…!"

Immediately, I sucked in a sharp breath.

It was very faint, but I could feel it. There was another button hidden behind the silver panel.

I leaned in close enough that my nose was nearly touching the panel, but there was absolutely no seam in the metal. In order to press it, I would have to risk the use of Incarnation.

Incarnation was the power of imagination. It would be very easy for me in my current state to move or change the shape of objects without using my hands. But that involved the process of looking at the object and using my imagination to shape it. That wouldn't be easy when the button was hidden behind the thick metal plate. If I was too clumsy with my application of power, I could easily break it.

What idiot came up with this horrible contraption? I grumbled to myself, using the barest minimum of imagination to see through the panel, envelop the invisible button, and press it.

There was a little thunk and rumble beneath our feet and then the hiss of a wind element being expelled below the floor.

The elevator began to rise, and Stica and Laurannei both exclaimed, "Wow!"

The automated levitating platform, or levitator, rose through the cathedral two or three times faster than the platform had in the old era when it was controlled manually. There was no floor readout, but a little bell rang with each floor that we passed.

It would have been trouble if someone else got on, but I guessed that pressing the hidden button would send it straight up like an express. We rose smoothly past the thirtieth floor, then the fortieth. The only downside was that, unlike the shaft from two hundred years ago, there were no windows here to offer a view of the outside.

The girl who operated the platform that took Eugeo and me up said that if she was ever released from her duty, she wanted to use the platform to fly freely through the sky.

She was probably no longer alive. As I counted the bell chimes, I closed my eyes and prayed that her wish had come true.

After a while, the levitator's ascent began to slow, and right as it came to a stop, the eightieth—er, seventy-ninth bell rang.

The doors slid open, revealing a dark hallway. There was no human presence here.

"Is this...the eightieth floor...?" Eolyne murmured, fear thick in his voice.

I gave him a prod. "Let's get off before the levitator starts moving back down."

"R...right."

He walked out of the box, followed by the other five of us. The hallway had not been cleaned in ages; thick white dust piled up on the floor, and our steps sent it wafting upward like smoke. Thankfully, dust in the Underworld was only treated like a visual effect and caused no distress if breathed in.

Alice ran forward several paces, kicking up dust, and shouted in a quavering voice, "I know it...This is the hallway that leads to the eightieth floor of Central Cathedral...the Cloudtop Garden!"

I remembered it, too. In perceived time, it was only two months ago that Eugeo and I had stepped off the levitating platform and walked this corridor.

At the time, I had told Eugeo, *We've come all this way to put a stop to Administrator. But that's not the end of it, Eugeo. The real problem is what comes after...*

Puzzled by my lack of specifics, Eugeo had asked, *Weren't we going to leave things up to Cardinal after we beat Administrator?*

I put off answering that question. I promised to tell him more after we'd taken back Alice, and I never got the chance to reveal the truth to him: that I was not a lost child of Vecta, but a human being from the real world by the name of Kazuto Kirigaya. That I wasn't a swordsman in that other world, but an ordinary, awkward child who had no real skills aside from gaming. That he was the only real friend I had who was a boy around my age.

"Hurry, Kirito!" Alice called, bringing me back to my senses. The five of them were already several yards ahead. I exhaled, squeezed the handle of the bag, and began to walk after them.

The large marble doors at the end of the short hallway seemed just as I remembered them, except for one thing that hadn't been there before: a strange metal pillar about three feet tall, coming up out of the ground just in front of the doors. The top was completely flat, with four nondescript slits in it. No other writing or buttons.

Alice gave the pillar a glance, then walked past it to the doors, as if she couldn't be bothered to waste time with such a thing.

"...I'm going to open this up," she declared, putting her hands on the pure-white marble. The force lifted a tiny amount of dust, but the life value of the door did not seem diminished in the least.

Even through the pilot's uniform, it was clear that Alice was putting all her effort into it. But the door did not budge. When Eugeo and I were here, we pushed it right open, but Alice, whose OC Authority was far higher than ours would have been back then, couldn't even get a creak with all of her strength.

"Rrh...gkh...!"

Asuna rushed up on Alice's left, and I dropped the bag so I could run and help. I put both hands on the right-side door and said, "Heave-ho!" With all three of us going together, I gave maximum effort.

It didn't move the tiniest bit.

The door was unbelievably tough. My OC number was a preposterous 129 right now. And that was affected by defeating the legendary Abyssal Horror, so Asuna and Alice could easily have risen in a similar manner as a consequence of that event.

If all three of us pushing together didn't make the slightest difference, then this wasn't just locked. There was some systematic power at work, some law of the world. I might be able to interfere with that using Incarnation but pushing a button in an elevator was one thing; using enough to destroy this door would undoubtedly set off all the Incarnameters in Centoria.

"Asuna, Alice," I said, calling them off. I took a step away from the door.

First Asuna, then Alice stopped pushing. The latter's pale cheeks were flushed painfully with longing and haste. I clapped her on the shoulder.

"I'm guessing that pillar behind us is the key...or the keyhole, I should say."

"But...we don't have any keys!" she wailed.

Asuna put a hand on her back next. "Let's take a look at it first. You've experienced many things like this in *ALO* by now, haven't you?"

"......Yes...," Alice admitted. We went back to the mysterious metal object.

Eolyne had already spent some time examining it. He took a step back and said, "Unfortunately, I have no idea what this is for."

"Based on the dust, I'm guessing it was installed here before you were born," I said, taking a look at the top of the pillar.

The metal panel was covered with dust, though not as much as the floor, with four slits cut into it. Each was about two inches long and a third of an inch wide...But upon closer inspection, I could see that the sizes were slightly different for each one. But even the smallest was about one inch by a quarter inch, which, if meant for a key, was a very large key, indeed. And there was no way to rotate it.

Was it not a key that was meant to go inside? Like a metal card...or something longer, like...

""""Swords!!"""" the three of us said in unison.

After sharing a quick look with them, I leaped over to the leather bag resting on the ground nearby. My fingers felt stiff as I undid the six buckles in order, threw the top open, and reached inside.

The first I grabbed was Radiant Light, which I handed to Asuna. Then I took out the Osmanthus Blade and gave it to Alice.

They stood before the pillar and drew their swords from the sheaths together. Behind them, Laurannei and Stica exclaimed with muted wonder.

I pulled out my two swords and shouted, "There should only be one slot each sword fits! Don't try to jam it into a spot that isn't right!"

"I know that!" Alice shouted back, holding the Osmanthus Blade upside down. She aimed for one of the slots, carefully putting the tip to the slot, and slid it in.

There was no certainty that the keys were our particular swords. Especially Alice's, since she had logged out of the Underworld before the Star King's reign began. In that sense, it might as well have been impossible to fashion a crevice that perfectly matched the Osmanthus Blade.

Despite the probability, I was certain these were the right swords. They *had* to be.

Shiiiing... With a smooth, cool sound, the golden blade sank into the depths of the pillar. Once about 70 percent of the blade was trapped inside the slot, there was a satisfying little *click*.

She took a few steps back without a word. Asuna took her place and put Radiant Light into another slot without a moment's hesitation. This one, too, sank about 70 percent in before it clicked.

I stuck both of my swords on my belt and stood up. There was a satisfying, familiar weight on me as I stood before the pillar. I grabbed each one backhanded and drew them, lifting the hilts high into the air.

In my right hand was the Night-Sky Blade. In my left was the Blue Rose Sword.

Behind me, I could sense Eolyne holding his breath. As a matter of fact, this would be the first time he ever saw the swords. But I stayed focused on the pillar and stepped forward.

Of the four slots in the line, Asuna's and Alice's swords occupied the two in the center. I pressed the tips of my two swords to the two outer slots and slowly but decisively slid them inside.

Both clicked together, and then a louder, more metallic *clank!* filled the hallway.

A golden line appeared down the middle of the marble doors behind the pillar.

They opened on their own, rumbling all the while. Bright light flooded into the gloomy corridor, filling my vision with white.

With a deeper rumble, the doors stopped at last.

Alice slipped past me and raced toward the overflowing golden light. Asuna followed her.

I let go of the swords' hilts and followed the two, the footsteps of Eolyne and the girls sounding behind my back. Once through the doorway, my nose was filled with a sweet and pleasant scent.

Light diffused and returned color to my eyes.

Green.

There was such a vivid cavalcade of green that it was difficult to remember we were inside a tall, tall tower. Just ahead was a green meadow covered with short, thick, soft grass, beyond which was a little brook and a wooden bridge crossing it that led to a gentle hill. This was the eightieth floor of Central Cathedral, the Cloud-top Garden.

The place where Eugeo and I were reunited with Alice the Integrity Knight and did battle.

Just like then, there was a single leafy tree standing atop the hill.

And at the roots…sitting down and leaning against the trunk, her eyes closed, was a girl.

In fact, it wasn't just one. Two other women stood to either side, as though guarding her.

Despite the way the gentle breeze rustled the grass that covered the hill, the occasional flower, and the branches overhead, the clothes and hair of the three figures did not move the slightest bit. They did not have the texture of the living. They had been petrified.

Even still, there was no mistaking the face of the sitting girl. She was more grown than how I remembered her, but I knew the gentle expression on those sleeping features.

Alice stumbled a step forward, then another, pressing her hands to her chest, and called out the figure's name, her voice thick with emotion.

"……Selka!!"

(To be continued)

AFTERWORD

Thank you for reading *Sword Art Online 25: Unital Ring IV*!

The Unital Ring arc has already reached its fourth volume (some would say it hasn't been that fast), and it feels like the story is really moving now. Mutasina and Eolyne were just making cameos in the previous volume, but they have a much greater presence in this book, and I think I've probably given you a good idea of what they're both about.

For now, events seem to be moving in parallel between *UR* and *UW*, but at some point, they are bound to approach one another and intersect. I hope you'll stick around as the Unital Ring arc moves closer to a climax!

(Spoilers for this volume to follow.)

In addition to writing new *Unital Ring* characters, I got to write a bunch of very familiar old names. Even I was surprised when the salamander who struck a deal with Kirito in the Fairy Dance arc showed up again, *with* a name and everything. I have a feeling that other *ALO* players will be showing up in dribs and drabs as the story proceeds.

As for the Underworld section, we did get a little glimpse of some of the central characters of the Alicization arc, if only as passing mentions. Of course, I had to end it right as Alice was about to...! But I'm sure we'll be finding out why the Integrity Knights were sealed next volume, along with other mysteries.

Look forward to it! And maybe we'll finally start to peel away the outer layer of that mysterious Commander Eolyne...

As for more personal circumstances, I'm writing this in October 2020, where the pandemic doesn't look likely to end anytime soon, and we're starting to put together a new kind of normal. While I think that the human adaptability on display is tremendous, there are many industries suffering heavily at this time (entertainment not least among them), and it seems like that's going to continue to have major consequences. The *SAO* world is one where the coronavirus pandemic never happened, or came and went, but while writing I can't help but be conscious sometimes that Kirito and everyone else aren't wearing masks...I'm hoping that I can find an appropriate middle ground for this that isn't overly optimistic *or* stressful.

And because of the pandemic...No, just kidding, because of my personal faults, I must apologize to my editor and abec for putting them through another horribly cramped schedule! I'll do better next time and give you more time to work! Hope to see you all next volume, folks!

Reki Kawahara—October 2020